The Write Connections

The Write Connections

2017 GLVWG Anthology

Greater Lehigh Valley Writers Group
Members

Greater Lehigh Valley Publishing Group

The Write Connections
2017 GLVWG Anthology

©2017 Greater Lehigh Valley Publishing Group (glvwg.org)

ISBN-13: 978-1542831918
ISBN-10: 1542831911

Acknowledgments

Anthology Chair
Bernadette Sukley
bernadettewsukley.com

Content/Developmental/Line Editing
John Evans, Phil Giunta, D.T. Krippene, David A. Miller, II

Copy Editing Staff
Pattie Giordani, Brenda Havens, Karen Rose, Dianna Sinovic

Book Design / Format / Cover Art
Christopher D. Ochs
christopherdochs.com

Cover art inset photographs used by permission from pixabay.com

Other Anthologies by
the Greater Lehigh Valley Writers Group

GLVWG Writes Stuff
2015

Write Here, Write Now
2016

Table of Contents

Poems

Authors

Introduction
The Founders

When the writing group you're looking for doesn't exist, you do the next best thing.

You create it.

Having attended lots of writing workshops, conferences and critique groups, Anne Keller and Lorraine Stanton cherry-picked the best qualities from each and set upon a shared goal of starting their own group for serious writers of book-length fiction. In 1993, the two friends started the Greater Lehigh Valley Fiction Writers Group. "We birthed it in Anne's living room," Stanton recalled. She had already published her first novel. Keller, meantime, had her hands full raising three young children while trying to squeeze in time to finish her first trilogy.

Within months of calling the first meeting to order, the group had swelled from five to a dozen members. As it grew, the group welcomed writers of everything from essays to short stories to poetry and mystery novels. That prompted a name change, dropping the word fiction to become the Greater Lehigh Valley Writers Group (GLVWG) for writers of all genres. Still true to its founders' mission, GLVWG acts as a network of support and offers resources that include lectures, programs, workshops, monthly Writers Cafe and annual Write Stuff Conference.

The anthology began as a self-publishing learning program for GLVWG members. It has become an opportunity for writers to follow the creative process to the happy conclusion. The final result is in your hands.

✝

Short Stories

Tea with Roses
Peggy Adamczyk

"Aunt Gretchen," Rose called, slamming a gray floral backpack down on the granite countertop. She yanked open an overhead cabinet, grabbed a glass, and filled it with ice. Using two fingers, she scooped a cube from the glass and popped it into her mouth.

"Aunt Gretchen," she shouted, setting the glass down on the counter. *Come on. I don't have time for this.*

Rose rummaged in the front pocket of the backpack for a blue elastic band. She pulled her brunette hair back into a ponytail and slipped into a kitchen chair to wait. *Going home is out of the question.*

Sneaking out of the house to party with her friends had been a stupid idea. How could she risk failing history class like that? If she failed, mom would take her cell phone, cancel her trip to France with the language club, and ground her for life. "Ugh!"

"Rose, dear, what is wrong now?" Aunt Gretchen asked, the kitchen's screen door screeching closed behind her. She placed a handful of cut flowers on the counter beside the sink and washed the dirt from her hands. Water splashed across the yellow-flowered apron protecting her blue knee-length dress.

Rose took a linen towel off the oven handle and handed it to Aunt Gretchen. "I have a history term paper due Monday. If it's not done, I flunk the class and Mom will cancel my trip to France."

"I see." Aunt Gretchen dropped the towel on the counter and took a vase off the windowsill. "Rose, you know better! Well, what is done is done." She arranged the flowers in the vase then added water. "Have you decided on a topic?"

"Not exactly."

Her aunt carried the flower arrangement into the dining room. Rose trailed behind her. *Can you please pay attention, Aunt Gretchen! Maybe this was a bad idea.*

Rose watched Aunt Gretchen from the doorjamb. Her great aunt hummed softly while she placed the vase on a crochet doily in the center of an antique maple dining table.

"Miss Timmons suggested, Influential Woman of the 1900s," said Rose, rapping her fingers on the doorjamb. "Aunt Gretchen, could you help? Can we get started now?"

Aunt Gretchen picked up a set of candlesticks off the hutch and looked over at her.

"Please," Rose added.

Aunt Gretchen smiled, set a candlestick down on each side of the vase, turned, opened a hutch drawer, grabbed two pink cloth napkins, and placed them on the table. "Tea first, it soothes one's mind. Please put the tea service out while I brew the tea."

Rose moved the old rose-patterned tea service from the hutch to the table. Aunt Gretchen carried the teapot into the kitchen. She slid into the chair to wait. *Tea! Aunt Gretchen wants tea and I need to write a term paper. Calm, be calm. Maybe telling Mom would have been a better idea.*

Aunt Gretchen strolled back into the dining room holding the steaming teapot. She poured them each a cup of tea, then set the pot down on the tray. "Did I ever tell you about my cousin, Eleanor?" She handed Rose a cup, removed an old yellow photo from the wall, and made herself comfortable in a chair.

"Thanks for the tea, but can we skip the family genealogy lesson. I really need help with my term paper," Rose said, trying not to sound too ungrateful.

"All things come in good time."

Where did she hear that before? Oh yeah! MOM!

Aunt Gretchen showed her the photo. "Eleanor is probably the favorite of all my cousins," she said.

Rose added two teaspoonfuls of sugar to her tea and clanked the spoon around in her cup. She tucked her feet underneath her, leaned in, studying the old photo. She read the caption aloud. "Campobello?"

"You look like Eleanor." Aunt Gretchen tapped the photo.

"Maybe her eyes . . . a little," Rose decided to play along. "Wait!" She leaned in closer to the image. "That's Franklin and Eleanor Roosevelt?"

"Oh dear! You thought I meant a different Eleanor?"

"I certainly didn't think you were talking about *the* Eleanor Roosevelt," Rose exclaimed.

"Sip your tea, dear. Cold tea will never do."

Rose slide her feet out from underneath her, leaned back in the chair, and sipped her tea. *Tea! Always the tea. Tea can't write my term paper or fly me to France. An old photo, stories—what good were they? Maybe I should have come clean with Mom.*

Aunt Gretchen smiled as if she knew what Rose was thinking. "Eleanor and Franklin cared for each other deeply," she said. "Like most people, they had a hard time showing it. I think Franklin's mother, Sara, complicated their relationship. Sara often took her role of matriarch to the point of being overbearing. Eleanor was often unsure and shy, and grateful for her help."

"Sara controlled the Roosevelts' lives!"

"Controlled may be too harsh a word. Remember, cultural norms for privileged society in the 1900s were very different from today. It wasn't unusual for a family's matriarch to run their son's household," Aunt Gretchen explained.

"That's crazy. My mother-in-law isn't going to order me around."

"Are you listening or commenting?"

Rose sighed. Clanking her spoon around her cup, she said, "Listening." She picked up her tea and took a sip.

Aunt Gretchen nodded, sipped her tea, and continued. "Franklin's family visited Campobello Island every summer of his life. The small lush island sits in the Bay of Fundy off the coast of Maine."

Rose leaned back in the chair and closed her eyes. She listened to Aunt Gretchen describe the island. She could feel the briny sea breeze waft across her face. Smell the freshly cut grass. See the red barn-like cottage, the flowering gardens, and the sweeping green lawns that lay before it. The more Aunt Gretchen talked the more hypnotic her words became.

Rose opened her eyes. She found herself sitting at a small lawn table with a rose-patterned teacup in front of her. Across from her, Aunt Gretchen was chatting with the woman in the photo. Tendrils of her dark-blond hair piled into a loose bun blew in the breeze. A watch, attached to a leather strap, was pinned to her white blouse.

Out on the lawn, people in strangely styled clothes mingled. The men wore white linen suits with sweater vests and baggy dress pants. The woman wore ruffled, boxy dresses and white gloves. Children dressed in colorful knickers and jumpers scurried past a brown-haired woman in a black skirt and white blouse walking around with a silver pitcher.

Rose shook her head, trying to clear it. She poked Aunt Gretchen's arm to see if she was real. *What was in that tea?*

The woman with the pitcher approached. "Madam, more tea?"

"Yes, thank you, Dolly." Eleanor held out her cup out. Dolly filled it from the silver pitcher.

Rose's palms grew sweaty. She scrubbed her hands dry on her thighs, bent over, tugged out a tuft of grass, and held it up to her nose. "Ah . . . choo."

"Bless you, child," Eleanor said.

Rose snapped her head up. *That answers one question.*

"You haven't caught a chill, have you?" asked Eleanor. "Facing a child's sickness when uncertainty surrounds Franklin's illness is too much to bear right now."

Aunt Gretchen nudged Rose with an elbow.

"No, ma'am," Rose responded.

Eleanor smiled, but there was no joy in her blue eyes.

Aunt Gretchen asked, "How is Franklin?"

"He lies in the front parlor either vacant to the world around him or defiant of his illness. The doctor is hopeful rest and convalescence will bring him back to us."

Her aunt talked with Eleanor as if they were old friends. Rose knew that was impossible. Eleanor Roosevelt lived before Aunt Gretchen was born.

"Franklin will do just fine," Aunt Gretchen assured Eleanor.

"You are such an optimist. I love that about you, Gretchen. The man is paralyzed and too stubborn to commit to a treatment until his mother arrives."

Maybe Aunt Gretchen is some old-school hippie type who used a hallucinogen on me. Well, I can play along if it gets my term paper finished on time. Wonder if Mom knew?

"Convince him," Rose said, playing along.

Eleanor and Aunt Gretchen both stared at her. Her aunt's brown eyes were as wide as Eleanor's blue ones. Rose felt a tightening in her throat. *Real or not, it's too late to back down now.*

"A wife should know what is best for her husband," Rose said, positive all Eleanor needed was to hear the truth from someone for once.

Aunt Gretchen placed her arm around Eleanor's shoulder and cleared her throat. "Perhaps children should remain silent when they don't understand what is happening."

Confused, Eleanor looked at Rose as if she had two heads.

"Eleanor," a woman yelled from the cottage porch, hands placed firmly on her hips. "Tea socials when my son lies abed helpless? Dolly, see to Eleanor's guests. They will depart . . . now. The family has business to address."

Dolly curtsied, set the silver pitcher down on a long table and spoke to the guests roaming the lawn. Some glanced at the cottage and walked off, others just left, but no one spoke a farewell to Eleanor. Rose thought it rude.

Rose asked, "Sara?"

"Indeed," Eleanor replied, walking toward the cottage.

Aunt Gretchen trailed behind her. "Mind what you say, Rose."

"Why?"

"History is as fragile and as easily changed as simply cracking the wrong egg."

She stared at Aunt Gretchen's back. *Sara seemed like a rotten egg you tossed in the trash bin. Wait! Is this place real?*

Rose darted after Aunt Gretchen, leaping up the steps two at a time to catch up. She missed the last step and tripped onto the porch. "OW," she cried, grabbing her ankle. *If the cottage isn't real, this pain sure is.*

Aunt Gretchen and Eleanor rushed out the screen door. She glanced up in time to see Sara following behind them, her brows furrowed.

"Child, you are too old for running up steps," Sara complained. "Put her in the sitting parlor. And see to a cold towel." She went back inside, letting the door bang shut behind her.

"Yes, Mother." Eleanor squatted, grabbed an elbow while Aunt Gretchen took the other one. They helped her into the parlor and made her comfortable in old-fashioned cushioned wicker chair. Aunt Gretchen lifted her foot onto the matching stool.

She caught Sara watching from the doorway. *I guess Sara believes Eleanor couldn't do anything right.*

"Tomorrow we will arrange Franklin's transfer back to New York to convalesce. Eleanor, you will close up the cottage and follow at your convenience. Afterward, we shall sell the townhouses at Hyde Park and retire to the country. There will be no more politicking."

"You can't do that . . . he can't do that," blurted Rose, positive she needed to say what was on her mind.

"Rose," Aunt Gretchen warned, resting a hand on her arm.

Rose didn't intend to stop her tirade. "Well, they can't and you know it."

"It's none of your concern, child. See to her needs and send them home. We haven't time for guests."

"Yes, Mother," Eleanor replied sadly.

Sara turned and left the parlor without another word.

Eleanor rang for the housekeeper. Turning back to her guests, she said, "Mother is right. Franklin needs rest. Sara knows what is best for the family."

Rose heard the sadness in Eleanor's voice and knew she disagreed with Sara. Eleanor's historical past existed already. Rose had learned about it in history class. Now she needed to convince the future President's wife to follow that course.

Rose said, "I think Sara is afraid Franklin's dependence on her will lessen if he continues politicking. What would Mr. Roosevelt want?"

Eleanor shook her head and looked down at her black pumps. "I must be fair with both of their needs."

"Doesn't your husband's need outweigh your mother-in-law's want?"

"Perhaps," Eleanor replied.

"Madam, you called?" the housekeeper said, entering the parlor.

"Yes, Dolly. A cold towel for the child's ankle and more hot tea." Eleanor rubbed her temples.

"Yes, madam." Dolly nodded and left.

The housekeeper's interruption gave Rose a few minutes to think. When she came up blank, she asked, "Aunt Gretchen?"

"No, this is your argument."

Rose should've expected that answer. Aunt Gretchen had been silent since she started discussing Franklin's future with Eleanor.

Eleanor's brow wrinkled in confusion.

Rose tapped her fist against her chin, stopping when she had a thought. "When you visited the sailors that were shell-shocked during the war, you found their treatment unacceptable, so you discovered a way to give them hope for the future."

Eleanor closed her eyes. Rose was sure she remembered that hospital ward. The emptiness she saw in those men's eyes. She went on. "Mr. Roosevelt's wounds came from an enemy he couldn't see—just like those soldiers. He probably feels just as lost. The only difference between him and those sailors is that you are Mr. Roosevelt's wife and you can fight for him directly. You can be his arms and legs when he is ready."

Eleanor brushed a wisp of hair out of her face. She stared out the oval window at the rolling surf in the bay. "I think Franklin would be bored in the country. Life is meant to be lived."

Rose could see the bay from where she sat. Slowly the bay was turning into a large rocky mudflat, full of tide pools. "Be Mr. Roosevelt's champion," she said. "You know what he wants even if he doesn't."

Eleanor faced Rose and Gretchen. A thin smile crept across her lips. "Franklin loves politics so. Do you believe such a simple thing could help Franklin's live his life again?" She sat in a chair opposite Rose.

Aunt Gretchen sat in another chair, in silence.

"I do," Rose said, knowing she was missing something. *What was it?*

"Franklin will take some convincing." A glimmer of hope crossed Eleanor's face.

"Articles," She blurted out. "You could write them. They would help Franklin." *What happened to finesse? Just glad I remembered.*

Gretchen nodded, obviously pleased she remembered about all of the influential articles Eleanor had written.

Eleanor smiled. "Mother will simply hate the idea."

"I am sure she will," Rose agreed.

The sound of wheels trundling into the parlor caught Eleanor's attention. She waved off the housekeeper, stood, and grabbed the cold towel from the dish and handed it to Rose.

Rose laid the towel over her ankle, while Eleanor poured tea and passed out the teacups. She closed her eyes, sipped the warm tea, enjoying the delicate flavor as it slipped down her throat. When Rose opened her eyes, she was staring at the photo in Aunt Gretchen's hand.

Aunt Gretchen smiled at me knowingly, and I had my term paper and trip to France.

✝

Wild Horses
Beverly Botelho

I smirk as the trainer bristles at my use of the word ornery.

"The horse is not ornery," she explains. "It knows what it should be doing. You merely have to discern and adapt to its wishes, then use that knowledge to work with it."

"Can I go for a solitary ride?" I ask.

"Someday."

As I consider her eyes, I realize she is looking behind me, around me, or through me. Everyone does this. We don't touch, we don't converse, we don't have contact of any kind, as if we are separated by panes of Plexiglas. I am trapped on one side, separated from those who interact with each other easily.

I want more than anything to be on the other side. I want to be running wild and free as the horses on the beach. I want to feel wind whipping through my mane—mares, stallions, ponies and steeds running with me.

But I am alone.

I talk. I move. I love. I act crazy as a chimp, playful as a pup, bubbly as a baby, brooding as a graduate student. But nothing I do gets through. I am invisible, alien, silent, separate. If I am wild, witty, or winsome, no one knows because they can't see, don't hear, won't discern.

An imageless mirror carries a memory of me. In it, I imagine my likeness. For comfort, I read Michio Kaku. He takes me to the places where I feel most comfortable. There's no place like home. That's when I realize that this world isn't real. These people are not friends.

This world I live in? A true universe, because there is only one of me—how can I break through to your side—how can I escape this puzzle of a prison?

Then I realize—everything is traveling the same path. True, we are separate, but we all move in a forward direction from one point to the next. It is the direction of the infinite—that great figure eight. Well, this is what I conceive—if I can play this path in time and in tune with you, then, sooner or later, we will meet in that center wasp's-waist of a place, the narrow tube where the soup of the pupa forms the adult being.

We are separate, but I see you. I run my finger over the membrane that keeps us apart. YES! The heart of the sacred place that traces its place in the heavens is throbbing right here. I push through as if I were a baby pushing through the womb into the world outside.

"So, take the reins," I hear the trainer say, her hands caressing mine. A human touch for the first time in my life.

I risk a smile and it is returned.

"I'd like to go for a solitary ride," I say.

"Soon."

The horse sighs as I stroke her side. I feel, I hope, I am on this side forever.

✝

Breakfast
Joy Crayton

He met her for the first time at Mother's funeral service. A dearth of planning resulted in no breakfast and no time to stop for coffee. In the church, he sat in the first pew, chafing in a suit and tie, eating the thickness of the air, the cloying stench of the flowers, the mourners' rank breath. They shuffled by, grasping his hands, banal expressions of sympathy dribbling from their lips.

He despised them. The gawkers and spectators. These nameless friends and friends of friends and the relatives whose sole talent was making appearances at weddings and funerals.

Irritation roiled within him. He wanted so much for this to be over. He wanted to eat. What he wouldn't give for just a piece of something sweet on his tongue.

A woman, the last of the mournful parade, clasped both his hands and slid a Ghirardelli chocolate square into his palm. He was startled out of his thoughts.

"You look like you could use a little something." Kind, knowing eyes peered at him from under long lashes.

She smiled, lips not parting, gently took him into her arms and hugged him.

Her touch was soft; her scent jasmine.

Nostrils opened, he filled his lungs, filled himself, with that scent. His scalp tingled. He wanted to hold her just a little longer but she released him.

Who is she? How did she know?

He tore the wrapper open and slid the square into his mouth. Bitter and

14

sweet, coffee and fruit filled him as the tears streamed down his cheeks, dripping off his chin.

✺

She was ephemeral. The memory of scent and touch. A taste of chocolate. A hint of jasmine. There and not there. It maddened him. He sought her in others and was rewarded for his efforts with the taste of bitter dregs. Intermittent lovers, reeking of patchouli, admonished him for eating meat, served interminable lectures for breakfast and no salt or butter with dinner.

When he stopped looking for her, she found him.

✺

It was morning. He was peckish and wanted something, but the coffee was tepid, tasting of cream and sugar, French roast flavor not bothering to make an appearance. Toast over and yet underdone. Two sides of the same piece of bread. Breakfast mocked him.

In the bedroom, she sat cross-legged on the bed. Her hair was reminiscent of Hungarian Komondors, her breasts little more than prepubescent. She once told him, through her laughter, that more than a mouthful would be superfluous.

He didn't laugh. That is to say, nothing approximating a laugh ever came out of him. Only a slight lift at the corners of the mouth, a sparkle in the eye. Mirth was there but muted.

There were those who didn't understand—thought he was mocking, smirking. They weren't paying attention, really. But she did. She peered into him. Through the gloaming into the beautiful day.

"I didn't smell the coffee, but I definitely smelled the toast." She smiled, reaching for him, brushing her hand along his thigh. "Wanna go out for breakfast?"

He didn't, but they did anyway.

∾

The wait staff knew her by name. Everyone knew her by name. She was light and air, hugging and kissing, greeting and being greeted, looking at those being spoken to. Her smile, bright and warm, matched her eyes. Comfortable with herself, her body moved effortlessly, seeming to flow through space and time. People gladly made of themselves an offering to her, which she graciously accepted.

He wanted to, but could not, offer himself freely.

He wanted to, but could not, subsume her.

At times he was not masterful, and then he became angry and rough.

But it hurt him when he was that way. Hurt him to think that he could not accept her freely as she did him. Hurt him to be disappointed that somehow, she was not angry or shamed or resentful when these things happened. When he was rough. It weighed on him. Made him feel as if he were curling over onto himself. *Into* himself.

"Are you all right? Is the coffee bad?"

"No. No. It's fine."

"Oh. I noticed you're not really tasting it."

So he put the cup to his lips, tipping the bottom up, waiting for the bitter rush of nothing. Anticipating the letdown.

It never came. Instead, there was richness and warmth, chocolate and fruit and silky sweetness. He forgot himself, and did not remember to be disappointed.

"Have another sip," she said.

And she was there on the bench next to him, waiting for him and he offered her his cup and she drank of it freely, easily. Somehow, in the sharing, he felt himself being lifted, relieved, as if he could finally straighten his back.

And he decided that she was all he wanted—all he needed.

✝

Dots
John Evans

The brick farmhouse hadn't changed much since I was a kid. The window frames needed some paint and a few slate shingles were missing. But, like the gray appearing at my temples, these subtle signs of aging went unnoticed over the years until seen on this sunny day.

Inside the house, things had aged as well. The furniture was worn and marred with nicks, the wallpaper faded and grease-stained by countless fingers feeling for light switches and doorknobs, and the footpaths on the Oriental rugs had become threadbare over the years.

The woman who lived in the house had also aged in gradual, unremarkable ways. She was older, slower, more frail and more careful and deliberate in her activities. What hadn't changed was the sparkle in her blue eyes that spoke of a sharp mind and an enthusiasm for life and all it held.

When she opened the door for me, however, she looked tired, worn out, defeated—holding herself steady behind her walker. Then she cocked her head to the side, crossed her arms, and said, "What do *you* want?"

"I came to see if you were all right."

She dropped her hands to the walker and said, "You came to see if I was dead. Do I look dead?"

"You look lovely."

"Liar . . . but come on in and give your old Aunt Mona a big hug." She smiled and held her arms wide. Her eyes sparkled once again.

I don't remember how we started the confrontational greeting, but it had become our custom. Her "accusation" that I was about to ask for something was a backhanded apology for the fact that she needed something. And my response was always an assurance that it was okay and that I still loved her—needed her.

She was my father's sister, my favorite aunt, and now my only family. A year ago she called once a month. Now she was calling twice a week. Her needs had increased as she lost her independence and her ability to fend for herself. And, yes, a few of her requests were simply an excuse to have someone to talk to.

I stepped into the house and gave her a peck on the cheek and a hug. It was a hug filled with brittle bones, dangerously delicate and fragile. Mona hitched her walker 180 degrees and chugged off toward the kitchen. The tennis balls on the back legs of the walker slid across the bare pine floor and the right front wheel squeaked painfully once per revolution.

"I'm so glad you were able to come today," she said.

"You said it was important."

I followed her through the living room with its dark furniture and a grandfather's clock that chopped off slices of life with its heavy, measured *chook . . . chook . . . chook*.

"It is," she said, navigating through the arched doorway. "I need you to check the sump pump and oil this wheel before I take a running dive off the back porch."

"I don't think you should do that," I said.

"And that's why it's important that you oil the damned wheel!"

At the kitchen table, she turned the walker so she could look me in the eyes. I was about to say something about a squeaking wheel getting the grease, but the look on her face stopped me.

"David, I'm losing my home."

We stared at each other for a long moment and then she side-stepped away from her walker and eased herself into a chair by the kitchen table. She nodded toward the chair across from her and I sat down.

"Pardon the mess," she said, waving a hand over a pile of manila file folders, envelopes with clasps, checkbooks, and ledgers. She sighed heavily and continued, "I don't know where to begin."

"You could start with your fixed income," I offered.

"And a dwindling savings account," she added. "That about sums it up."

Another long silence followed as we stared at nothing. Finally, she said, "Thirsty? I made a pitcher of mint tea. It's in the fridge."

I went to the cupboard and helped myself to a glass.

"Make it two," she said.

As I added ice to the glasses and poured out the tea, she continued. "I've been living on one floor here. I can barely keep up with the housework—cleaning, laundry, tending my flowers. And I can't be calling you every time I need to climb a stepstool. And, seriously, I'm bored to death with crossword puzzles and reading mysteries."

"Maybe you should get some help—have a nurse stop in. You shouldn't be alone."

Mona held up her medallion—a plastic rectangle on the chain around her neck. She pretended to press the blue button in the center.

"I've fallen and I can't get up!" she cried and smiled weakly. "The fact of the matter is that if I do fall, I may decide not to get up. That would solve everything."

"Talk like that again, and you won't need to take a dive off the back porch—I'll give you a push."

She picked up an envelope labeled "Last Will and Testament" and waved it at me. "You push me off the porch, you'll get the Big House—not the farmhouse."

We laughed and settled into another silence, marred only by the *chook . . . chook . . . chook* in the other room.

"But the house . . ."

"That's why I called you." She sipped her tea, stirred the ice cubes with a spoon and took another sip. "It's time I go to Country Care. I hear the staff is good and so is the food. There's plenty to do and I'll have all kinds of people to talk to—people my age with my interests. The thing is . . . I'll have to sell the house. I wanted you to get everything. I don't want to spend your inheritance on a nursing home, but it's time."

"You should see a lawyer. They call it protecting your assets. They're good at it."

She rattled the ice cubes and drained the last few drops of tea from her glass. "Would you like some more?" she asked, as if she were going to serve. I nodded and went to the refrigerator for the pitcher. I filled our glasses and held one out to her.

She took her glass in two hands and gave me a steady look.

"Yes, they've helped me plenty, but they can't help me with this. I've seen to it that you get my estate—whatever's left of it. But I think there's more." She pointed to the pile of folders. "I may have more than anyone knows."

She put her glass down. "Years ago, Uncle Paul came into a little money —an inheritance from his sister. He put it all in a 401(k). Over the years it grew to nearly a half million dollars. We thought we had it made. And then the housing bubble broke. We lost it all—or so I thought. Now I'm not so sure."

She picked up a file and pulled out a page. "These statements are from Edward Jones. The last one is dated May 2007." She held the paper away from her and squinted at it. "Four hundred and ninety-seven thousand bucks. Not bad. This was a few months before things fell apart. But this is the last statement I have. No reports showing a rapid drop in value, no closing statement or cancellation notice. The statements stopped with this one—and, remember, Paul kept everything."

I took the statement and looked at it, specifically at the value—four hundred ninety-seven thousand, eight hundred seventy-two dollars and seventeen cents. I had no idea they had that much money.

"Then there's this." She flipped a pamphlet on the table in front of me like she was dealing cards. It spun to a stop and I read the heading, "Investing in Gold! Smart Choices."

"Paul met some drunk down at Patrick's Pub," she continued. "The guy ranted about the stock market—said it was going to crash. He gave Paul that pamphlet."

She took a sip of tea. "And now it's time to check the sump pump."

I was a little shocked at this sudden change of topic, but recovered to ask, "Are you getting water in your cellar?"

She shook her head. "We've never had water in the cellar. And that's rare for an old farmhouse. She flipped another brochure in front of me, an advertisement for a submersible sump pump. "This was in the same file with the gold pamphlet. Shortly after he met the drunk, Paul said we needed a sump pump—for a rainy day." She used air quotes for emphasis. "Rainy day, indeed." She paused and rattled the ice cubes in the glass. "He spent an entire day digging in the cellar and when he was done, he came up all sweaty, but smiling. 'It's done,' he said. 'Let it rain.' And then he went to bed. That was the last it was mentioned. He died three weeks later. About a month after that, the news was all about the housing bubble breaking."

Mona tilted her head back and drained the tea filtering down through the ice cubes. "David, these are clues. How good are you at connecting the dots?"

"I'll go get the pick and shovel," I said.

Mona nodded with a weak smile and I rose to go outside. I found the tools in the garden shed and went around to the side of the house and pulled open the wooden doors to the cellar steps. As I brushed my way through the cobwebs, the light went on. "Thanks, Aunt Mona," I shouted.

"The least I could do," she said from somewhere in the house.

The cellar was dank and musty, with cobwebs worthy of Dracula's castle. It was empty except for a rusty oil tank, a furnace on a slab of concrete, and a chest freezer in the far corner—the cord and plug snaking out from the side with no outlet in sight.

"Aunt Mona," I shouted toward the stairs to the kitchen. "You don't have a sump pump."

I heard the squeak, squeak of her walker traversing the floor above. "I thought not," she said. "Do you see any signs of digging?"

I looked around the packed earth floor and found nothing. "Not yet.

The only place could be under the freezer."

"Freezer?"

"There's a freezer down here. Unplugged."

"What's in it?"

I opened the lid and found a strange collection of tools and electric motors, each one heavier than the last, from a circular saw to an anvil right out of a Road Runner cartoon.

"It's packed with enough scrap metal to sink a barge," I said.

"Empty it. I'll get you some more tea. You're going to need it." And I heard her squeak off toward the refrigerator.

It took a half hour to move the contents of the freezer to the middle of the cellar. When I muscled the freezer out of the corner, I found a patch of floor two feet by four feet that had been disturbed. The earth floor of the cellar was layered with clay and tamped down to a smooth surface with a dull sheen. The patch was also tamped down, but not as well. It was obvious someone had dug a hole in that spot. Eureka!

I used the pick to break through the clay, and my heart sank—shale. There is nothing worse than shoveling shale. I attached my ear buds to my phone and selected a playlist to settle into a long, hard task. After a half hour of wrestling with the shovel, my shirt was wet and I took it off. The air was heavy and stagnant. I needed tea breaks every ten minutes, and with every break, I found new dots to connect. Why the sudden end to statements? Maybe Paul switched to e-statements. Maybe he tore the last ones up in disgust.

More digging. I was down a foot and out of tea. I called for more, and I heard Aunt Mona squeaking around above as she prepared another pitcher. While I waited, I did some Internet searching. How much gold could Uncle Paul buy for a half million? A quick Google search revealed that he could buy just over 45 pounds, worth about $893,000 in today's market.

I heard the cellar door to the kitchen open. "David?" Aunt Mona called and I went up and took the sweating pitcher from her.

"How's it going, David?"

"It's hot work, but it's going well. Haven't found anything—yet."

"When you do, holler. I'm going to water some flowers out back and lie down awhile."

I returned to the hole and my playlist. I peered in for a moment and went at it for another hour, taking it slow and stopping often. "Why so deep?" I asked myself, and had another thought. I did another search and calculation. A block of gold worth $893,000 would fit into a cigar box. This didn't make sense. Another half hour of digging got me to unbroken shale, the bottom of the pit, but no gold. Another dot. Either Uncle Paul didn't withdraw his money in time or he buried it elsewhere. Maybe the hole really was for a sump pump he decided he didn't need—*Let it rain.* Or maybe he needed a place to bury his financial advisor. I chuckled at the thought.

And as I stood looking into the hole with Bruce Springsteen blasting in my ears, I felt a presence near me. I turned and jumped at the sight a police officer standing before me. I tore the ear buds from my head.

"Put the shovel down," he said.

I let it slide from my hand and it fell into the hole.

"I need you to turn around and place your hands behind you."

I turned and my mind raced. Was hoarding gold illegal?

"Officer, what's . . . ?" The cuffs clamped painfully around my wrists.

"Mrs. Henry . . ." he said and stopped.

"She's my aunt. What's going on?" I twisted my head around to see him.

"We're responding to a medical alert. Mrs. Henry fell out back . . ." he paused and looked around the cellar, "or was pushed."

"Is she . . . ?"

"I'm sorry," he said in a tone lacking empathy.

His eyes continued darting around the cellar at the freezer, the scrap metal, the hole, and the shovel.

I closed my eyes, knowing he had just connected his own set of dots—a body, a grave, and a gravedigger whose name would be found in the victim's last will and testament as the sole beneficiary.

Dots—lousy, freaking dots.

✝

Once More, With Feeling
Phil Giunta

Alone in the darkness, the man gazed up at the stars. Several yards away, the ocean propelled itself upon the sand, retreated, and thrust forward again. The rhythm was soothing and the man imagined his worries drifting out to sea, never to return.

If only it were so.

Before moving to this coastal town seven years ago, he had come here only for summer vacations. Back then, he would have balked at the idea of lying alone on the beach at night rather than crawling bars or strolling the boardwalk.

Always in motion.

Never living in the moment.

Those days were a blur now—faded memories from another man's life. Tonight, on the eve of his forty-fifth birthday, he concerned himself only with the full moon, the stars, and the surf. Together, they worked a certain magic of sight and sound that temporarily dispelled the depression and anxiety that had consumed him for decades. Though he'd become a household name, and was able to retire on a small fortune from the sale of his social media company, he had never truly felt alive—more like an automaton, a robot. Going through the motions of life, without actually living.

Always doing.

Never *feeling.*

Those days of empire building had been a necessary evil—a means to an end. Now, as he lay here, childless and unmarried, with terminal cancer eating away at his brain, the man was left with only his regrets for

25

companionship. Any morning on this secluded beach could be his final chance to cast them aside and capture that elusive perfect moment when the weight of his sorrows would be lifted, allowing him to feel truly alive before the end. *Lord, should I draw my final breath tonight, please grant me that moment.*

"Mind if I join you?"

She spoke in a soft tone as if to avoid startling him, but he'd anticipated her arrival. Without averting his gaze from the heavens, he waved a hand toward the towel he'd laid out beside him earlier. She lowered herself gracefully, digging her perfect toes into the sand, before stretching out. She never aged. She'd been with the man through his entire life, yet she appeared no older than the last time he saw her when he was ten—although she hadn't worn a bikini back then. *Now if that's the last thing I see, maybe I'll die a happy man after all.*

"Not that I'm complaining," the man began, "but why are you wearing that?"

"I always dress for the occasion. This seemed appropriate given our surroundings."

"But it's nighttime."

"Does that matter?"

With a grin, the man shrugged. "Not to me." A moment of silence passed between them before he continued. "I suppose a 'thank you' is in order."

"For?"

He smiled wanly. "Despite my imminent—and utterly *premature*—demise, I wouldn't have made it *this* far if it weren't for you."

She turned her face to the sky. "Guiding you through adulthood was actually easier than expected. It was at the beginning of your life when I believe I failed you."

"What do you mean?"

"You've battled terrible depression ever since you were a child. As a teenager, you attempted suicide three times—"

The man held up a hand. "But you were there to stop me each time. You did your job."

"If I had done my job, you never would have reached that point."

The man was surprised at her sharp tone.

She paused as if to compose herself. In a softer voice, she continued. "When you were a child, my instructions were to protect you and keep you safe from injury wherever you went. I did not anticipate what would happen to you at the hands of others, the very people who should have loved you most."

The man shrugged. "So I got banged up a little, just like lots of other kids. That wasn't your fault. *You* didn't inflict that pain. The only actions you're responsible for are your own."

She scooped up a handful of sand. Dull grains in her palm sparkled like flecks of diamond as they slipped through her slender, divine fingers. "What about my *inaction*? After your parents divorced when you were five and everything fell apart, I was . . . caught off-guard."

"You and me both, gorgeous."

"I was powerless to intervene the night your mother nearly beat you to death in her blind rage after your father maligned her during the custody hearing. Then a year later, I tried in vain to stop your father from throwing you down the stairs over some trivial insult from your mother. I wasn't prepared for him to take it out on you. The only thing I could do was comfort you after the fact and help heal your wounds as quickly as possible.

"But there was nothing I could do to take away the *emotional* pain. That was . . . beyond my ability. You were left to find your own way through the fear and darkness in your mind where I could not reach you. That remains so, even now."

He narrowed his eyes and shot her a sidelong glance. "You know, I *was* trying to have a pleasant time out here. Look, I survived all that and a lot more, and I'm not the only one in the world who had it rough growing up. Plenty of people have baggage, some more than others." Despite the throbbing in his head, he turned on his side and gazed at this ethereal beauty, amazed at her flawless skin, obvious even under the stark glow of a full moon. She'd let down her long brown hair since the last time he'd seen her. It cascaded around her head, flowing off the edges of the beach towel. "Where's all this self-reproach coming from, anyway? You've had other charges before me, right? They couldn't have all been easy."

She shook her head. "For everything there is a first time. That includes you. I was so naïve in the beginning."

The man didn't know what to say. He'd never been anyone's first before. There was something special about having an angel all to yourself. "Well, life's a learning experience, even for you. You'll do better with your next one. How many does it take before you earn your wings?"

She smiled, more radiant than a summer sunrise. "We don't actually get wings, you know. That's just how we're depicted by your artists and filmmakers."

"Good, because from what I can see, you have a lovely back." *And everything else.*

She raised an eyebrow. "I can read your thoughts, you know."

Stifling a gasp, he turned his face away and stared at the sky. Moving his head right or left had become agony since the tumor began growing at the base of his neck. "Yeah, well, in my condition, I'm long past caring about that."

"But you're still not at peace." She sat up and faced him, folding her legs in a lotus position. "The damage was done too long ago."

On the horizon, black began its daily surrender to blue as the man replied. "Some of us mortals carry our baggage to the grave. Honestly, I think that's the only worldly possession we *can* take with us. I've never known what it's like to live without depression, without anxiety, or fear. I spent so many nights hoping I'd die in my sleep rather than wake up another day feeling like that. I sometimes wonder if I kept busy all of my life as a way of ignoring my pain. I had no real passion for my career; it was just something I did to make money. I lived to work, instead of working to live."

He winced as pain flared through his skull like a shockwave. When it finally passed, he continued. "There's not a day that goes by when I wouldn't trade it all for the chance to be happy, to fall in love, maybe start a family, but . . . it's too late now. Today, I just want to live in the moment before all of my moments are gone." The man's voice broke and his vision clouded as moisture welled up in his eyes. He averted his gaze to the sunrise as it set fire to rippling clouds. Gossamer flames drifted across a slowly waking sky. During all those past summers, mornings had been spent running along the beach to stay fit and combat the stress of an angst-ridden life. There had never been time to stop and bask in the light of a new day.

Always in motion.

It was all a blur now.

The angel unfolded her legs and lay beside him. "It's never too late." She kissed him on the forehead and retreated from view, leaving only an expanse of unbroken azure above him. The warmth of the sun—or was it her touch? —the rhythm of the waves, the shriek of distant seagulls.

So this is what life feels like.

"Live in this moment . . ." she whispered.

Peace filled the man's heart as the world faded away.

～

"Who are you?" The little girl frowned as she propelled herself ever higher on the backyard swing.

Silently emerging from a field of tall corn surrounding the house and yard, the woman took a seat on the neighboring swing and smiled. "I'm your guardian angel, and I think you should take it easy on that swing before you hurt yourself, okay?"

The girl dragged the toes of her sneakers into the dirt. It took two passes to bring herself to a full stop. "My mom and dad told me everyone has a guardian angel, but I didn't believe them."

"And yet, here I am. Your mom and dad are wonderful people. They work hard and they love you very much. That should make my job a lot easier this time."

"What?"

"Well, you see, I was assigned to you the moment you were born. I'm here to help you live a long and happy life by keeping you safe no matter where you go in the world."

The girl narrowed her eyes and shot her a sidelong glance. "I don't see your wings. You ever do this before?"

The angel couldn't help but smile. *Some things never change.*

The girl's skeptical expression softened as the angel laughed. "Only once, but I learned a lot. In fact, you could say this is a second chance—for both of us."

✝

Mementos
Keith Keffer

I couldn't wait to wiggle my toes in the damp grass covering their graves. Yeah, I know it sounds weird, and it probably is to most people, but not for me. When my bare skin touches the ground, I feel closer to them. It reminds me of our days together, of the good times we shared. Those days are gone, but the memories remain.

No one can take those away from me.

The headlights of the black SUV glide across the road, but they don't reach very far. The world is an impenetrable wall of white, as the fog absorbs the light. I love the morning fog. It's a mask that conceals the truth. Even the sounds are different. That's why I picked this place to lay them to rest. Once the fog rolls in, there is nothing to distract me. The morning is the best time to visit, before the sun comes up. That's when the fog is at its densest. I never get to stay too long, but while I'm here the burdens of life fade away. It's the only time I feel at peace.

My driver, David, gripped the steering wheel with both hands. Occasionally, he would glance my way in the rear-view mirror to make sure I was still in the backseat, but the last time he did that we hit a pothole. The car had swerved, nearly clipping a tree. After that, his eyes remained focused ahead as we bumped our way over the uneven road.

The turn would be coming soon, but David didn't know that. This was all new to him. Just one of the secrets I had kept from him. He waited quietly for me to tell him when to make a right. Except for my directions, we remained silent. That was fine with me. I preferred my solitude. David, on the other hand, could easily spend hours asking me questions, but today was different. Today, he was content to let me ride in peace. The only sound came from the hiss of air flowing through the car's heater, and even that was low.

I scooted closer to the passenger side window, careful not to spill the contents of the battered cardboard box resting on my lap. It was a little larger than a shoebox, but not as large as those storage boxes you pick up at the office supply store. David had wanted to keep the box in the front seat, next to him, but I wouldn't hear of it. I always carried it with me when I visited the graves, and that wasn't going to change today. He finally relented, and I've held the box with both hands ever since.

That couldn't have been easy for him. David is a take-charge kind of guy, and he likes to be the one calling the shots. This time, I was the one in the figurative driver's seat. This is *my* journey, and if he wanted to join me, he had to follow *my* rules.

I caressed the box with one hand as I looked out the window for the upcoming turn. The keepsakes stored inside where all that I had to remind me of what they'd been like when they were still alive. I had peeked inside once, and only once, to make sure everything was there. A lock of hair wrapped in a blue ribbon. A gold ring on a slender chain. A keychain with a peace symbol on it. They were there, right on top, carefully packaged in individual plastic bags. I liked the bags. They did their best to protect each memento. There were more than just the three, lots more. Each one had been carefully labeled with a number and a description.

That had been David's work. He, or someone he worked with, had spent hours carefully cataloging each one. In some ways, I think he treasured them even more than I did. He'd had so many questions about each one that I thought he would never tire of asking them.

In the silence of the car ride, I realized I had a question for him. "Why are *you* driving?"

Anyone could have sat in the driver's seat for this journey. It didn't have to be him. As far as I knew, he had never met any of them in person. Everything he learned came second hand.

He didn't answer. Maybe he was lost in his own thoughts. Maybe he didn't hear me. I was about to ask him again when he cleared his throat.

"We all need closure."

"Even you?" I said, curious in spite of myself.

He shrugged while keeping both hands on the steering wheel. "After today, everyone will be able to move on. That includes me." He glanced in the rear-view mirror and his blue eyes met mine for only a second before looking away. "The only one who won't move on is you. Nothing will change for you."

"That hardly seems right," I said. "I was hoping to get something out of this too."

David laughed. For as long as I've known him, I've only heard him laugh three times. It wasn't a pleasant noise. It sounded like a squirrel choking on a nut.

"This was your idea," he said. "I'm sure you know exactly what you'll be getting out of this, and in a way, I'm glad I don't know what it is."

"Are you sure? Aren't you even a little curious? You're always looking for answers, David. Maybe my reasons will give you some."

"I used to think that," said David, "but not anymore. Once we're done here, I can wash my hands of all this."

"You want to wash your hands, David? Does working with me make you feel unclean?"

"Every day."

I stared at David. That might be the first time he's ever expressed his dislike of me. I knew it was there. Our relationship isn't the type sitcoms are based on. We have nothing in common except for our interest in the graves we were about to visit.

The turn flashed past my window. It wasn't so much a side road as a pair of ruts. David probably never saw them. They were easy to miss even if you knew what to look for.

"There it is," I said. "We just passed it."

David hit the brakes, and the SUV slid to a stop. I rocked forward before my seat belt caught me and pulled me back.

"Where?" he said. In the thick fog, the side road was nearly invisible.

"About thirty feet back, on the right."

David swore and put the SUV into reverse. We had to wait as the line of cars behind us followed his example and started to back up. I had counted at least two sets of headlights, but there might have been more. It took almost ten minutes before we had moved far enough back to find the trail again.

"Really?" said David as he studied the path before him. "That's not a road."

"Privacy is very important to me, David. I thought you would have realized that by now."

He grunted and put the SUV into 4-wheel drive before making the turn.

"It's not far," I said. "Just beyond that line of trees." Obscured by the fog, the trees made me think of the towering wall surrounding some sort of medieval fortress. In a way that was appropriate. They marked the border of my private sanctuary.

I rocked side to side as the tires hit each dip in the trail, but even if our path had been as smooth as glass, I would have been bouncing in my seat. It had been over three years since the last time I was here, and I was more excited than a kid on the last day of school. We were almost there.

The car rolled forward so slowly that I was tempted to jump out and walk the rest of the way. I would have, except that the doors were locked and there was no way David was going to open them for me until we stopped. Only a few more seconds, then I'd be with them again.

I kicked off my sneakers. It only took a slight nudge against the heel for them to slide off since they didn't have any laces. The carpeting under the back seat felt dry and brittle against my bare feet.

The car stopped.

"Is this it?" asked David.

I smiled and nodded. "Yes. Yes." I pressed my nose against the glass of the window.

Keith Keffer

The clearing was lit up like Christmas. Flashes of red and blue danced across the trees as the other cars pulled up alongside of us, their headlights creating halos of light in the fog. It was as if the spirits of the dead had come to greet me.

A shadow passed in front of my window followed by the click of a lock. A uniformed officer opened the door, and I swung my legs out of the car, careful not to get tangled in the chains around my ankles. My bare feet touched the cold, damp grass, and I shivered. I couldn't wait to walk over their graves. David appeared at my side and pulled me the rest of the way out of the car.

"This way," I said. It was awkward walking while holding my box. My handcuffs chafed against the cardboard, threatening to tear open the side with each step.

I paused to open the box. After fumbling with the lid, I extracted one of the small, plastic bags. With it clenched tightly in one hand, I held out the box to David. "Would you mind carrying this for me?"

He fixed the lid, then took the box in both hands. He held it as carefully as I would have. "What about that one?" he said, indicating the bag I still carried.

"We'll visit him first." It was the keychain with the peace symbol. The words 'Allen Richards, Age: 62, Missing: 06/17/11' were neatly typed on the tag glued to the bag. Mr. Richards had been on his way home from visiting his grandkids when I met him. For an old guy, he had been a fighter. He probably would have gotten away if his heart hadn't given out. Then again, considering what I had planned for him, maybe he did get away after all.

Mr. Richards was my second victim. The first had been an accident. I had been alone and just wanted to connect with someone, anyone. I swear all I wanted to do was to talk, but she panicked and started screaming. I guess I panicked too. I just wanted her to be quiet, and after a few seconds she was.

At that moment, when the life faded from her eyes, she and I were one. I

35

had never felt so close to anything or anyone in my entire life as I did in that instant. It had changed me, made me a new man, happy and confident for a change. It didn't last. After a few months, I began to withdraw into myself. Fear about what I had done began to gnaw at me. I knew it was only a matter of time before I was going to be caught, but I couldn't let that happen without trying to regain that sense of purpose once more.

That was where Mr. Richards came into my life. His death was sudden, beyond my control. It lacked the connection I had established with my first.

So, I tried again. And again. Each time trying to recreate the spark of the first time.

I stopped and closed my eyes, curling my toes in the grass. A chill flowed through me. At my feet sat a red brick with the number two etched into it. I opened my eyes and knelt, feeling the dampness soak into my knee as I placed the evidence bag on the marker.

With a smile, I got back to my feet and reached for the next bag. Homicide Detective David Myers and I would be at this for a while.

✝

Wren Boy
Charles Kiernan

F riday night. Time to clean the apartment.

Melissa drags the Hoover from its assigned place in the bedroom closet, plugging it into the living room socket. From there it will unroll its cord as needed to reach the bedroom, living room, but not quite the farthest corner of the kitchenette.

Today she elects to give special attention to the sofa. She removes the brush attachment, strokes the furniture's sides with the wand, picks off the cushions, thoroughly cleaning and stacking them on the coffee table, then thrusts the wand into the sofa's crevices.

Finishing that, she follows the wand along every corner and ceiling line, searching for spider webs—none exist in her apartment.

Wiggling the brush attachment back onto the end of the wand, she sweeps the spines and tops of her beloved books in their cases. She longs for bookcases with glass doors to enshrine them, but the books continue to suffer because of her modest income.

One of the books, *The Folklore of Birds,* lies sideways across the others, not yet finding it place among them. She bought it a week ago at a yard sale, fifty cents. Melissa sits on her stuffed ottoman, switching off the Hoover, letting the hose snake about her feet as she picks up the book, perusing its pages.

Her eyes fall upon an image, a photo of three boys face the camera, each wearing a wild hat, one is a flute player, flanked by drum players. Behind them stretches a muddy road and little else. The photo is dated as taken in Athea, 1946.

Melissa's cell phone chimes and vibrates in her pocket, Beethoven's Fifth as its ringtone.

"Hello?"

"There, the boy on the right holding the drum—the bodhrán—that's me."

Melissa takes the phone from her ear and stares at it. Looking out her window she sees the solid brick wall of the building next to her. No one can be spying on her.

"What are you doing?" she says into the phone.

"We are wren boys." He addresses the photo, not her question. The soft, polite voice holds seriousness and sadness.

"Wren boys?"

"Saint Stephen's Day, after Christmas, we lads would parade a poor dead wren around from house to house, declaring the bird to be the king, asking for treats, and playing truly horrible renditions of songs on our instruments."

Melissa laughs. It's the sadness in his voice to which Melissa responds, suspending her question about who is on the other end.

"Please turn to page 156," the Wren Boy says.

Melissa pages through the green bound book, buying into this odd adventure. There appears a page with musical staff notations and lyrics.

"What is this?" she asks.

"That is the song we sang. I barely remember the words."

The choir girl in Melissa rises up. By sight, she recognizes the tune although not the lyrics. "I think I can sing it to you."

"Oh, would you?"

Melissa clears her voice.

> "The wren, the wren, the king of all birds,
> on Saint Stephen's Day was caught in the furze.
> Up with the holly and ivy tree,

where all the birds will sing to me.
"Knock at the knocker, ring at the bell,
please gi's a copper for singing so well,
singing so well, singing so well.
Please gi's a copper for singing so well.
"God bless the mistress of the house,
a golden chain around her neck,
and if she's sick or if she's sore,
the Lord have mercy on her soul.
"Knock at the knocker, ring at the bell,
please gi's a copper for singing so well,
singing so well, singing so well.
Please gi's a copper for singing so well."

"Oh, thank you. You sang it so much better than we. That was the song we sang to her."

"Her?"

"Yes, this young girl and her mother stood on their stoop and laughed and laughed at our attempt to be musicians. They were new to the village and I loved her at once.

"For years, every Saint Stephen's Day we'd come mumming, and I knew I would always see her then, I rarely saw her otherwise, she not attending our school. My heart pattered the whole time, and I recall my sadness when we moved on to the next house.

"Then came that special summer. We were in our teens, and in the evenings we'd meet in the village park, called the Giant's Garden, for hours. We both knew our affections were made of glass, destined to shatter. Only our secret kept us in our own little bubble, apart from the rest of the world."

"What secret?" Melissa frowns.

"Oh, she was Catholic and I, Protestant. I at least middle class, but she lower. My father, a dyed in the wool Loyalist, I knew would never approve.

One evening we sat on our bench, our hands touching. 'I need to ask you,' she was saying when her eyes darted away from me and her expression froze. I smelled my father's cologne a moment before I felt his beefy hand upon my shoulder, whirling me around.

"'How could you?' he said to me. I still see his is eyes boring into me."

Melissa draws in a breath in sympathy. He continues.

"In my mind's memory, he picked me up and carried me off. I am sure I remained on my feet, nonetheless, he propelled me away. What I know, is when I looked back at her, whom my father never addressed, as he might not address an animal, I saw alarm for me, shock for us, and sadness for herself emanating from her being. I cannot let that be my lasting memory of her."

"That's so sad. What did your father do?" Melissa wiped at a tear welling at the corner of her eye.

"Father did not attack my affections for her, but declared me, in totality worthless, and insensitive to the greater struggle. He made me doubt myself. By fall, I attended a boy's boarding school, outside of London no less. I never saw her again.

"Years later, after I had sorted out my father's prejudices, and despite the times being in the middle of 'The Troubles,' I tried to find her again. Where she had lived was still occupied by Catholics, but they knew nothing of who lived there before them. I talked to longtime residents. They said nothing. Yet, I knew they knew. They would not say. I fear she entered into prostitution, hence the silence.

"Still, to my mind, she is sacred. The jewel I preserved for all these years, unblemished, are those summer nights in the Giant's Garden."

"What did she look like?"

"I remember her ivory skin, framed by long black hair. She had lips that smiled with a touch of deviltry behind them, and blue eyes as clear as wet glass. And a summer frock she loved to wear, white with black trim, like her very skin and hair.

"I recall little of what we said to each other, although we talked and talked. But I remember listening to the bell-like tones in her voice. Her talk sounded more like a church carillon to me."

"That's lovely."

"Well, sometimes I suspect my memory has glorified her, but that's my father's side of my brain talking. The part of my brain that is me, alone, knows the truth of my image of her."

"What happened to you afterward?"

"I married. We had children. I held a decent job. A good life. But, now that I am gone, my thoughts return to her. I think of the 'what could have beens'. What was lost when my father grabbed me off the park bench. If I were a book, there'd be pages ripped from an early chapter."

He pauses, then continues. "But, my dear, what of you?"

"Me?" Melissa's hand goes to her heart. "I'm . . . I'm fine. You need not worry . . ."

The cell phone beeps—low battery—then turns itself off.

"No, wait!" She holds the cell staring at it for a moment.

Then she sets it down on top of the bookcase, beside her world globe and a framed picture of her parents.

"What could have beens," she repeats.

Melissa unplugs the Hoover, returning it to the bedroom closet. Standing at the closet door, she passes her hand along her dresses, landing on a short sleeve, green one. She puts it on, looks at herself in the closet door mirror, then changes into the sleeveless red dress.

Collecting her keys from the carnival glass bowl on the living room side stand, she goes down the short foyer to her apartment door, opens the dead bolt, and re-locks it behind her.

It is, after all, a summer evening.

✝

Roots And Branches
Gisela Leck

Whether you like it, fight it, accept it or simply ignore it, time never stands still. We all get older.

I had driven for two hours straight and my knees felt as stiff as an old varsity football jacket. I unbuckled my seat belt and took a deep breath. Fifteen years is a long time, I thought. How do you start a conversation after not speaking for a decade and a half?

Always a fast walker, I forced myself to take slow steps to delay meeting my once former best friend and college roommate, but the entrance to the outdoor mall where we agreed to meet was just a stone's throw away. An elderly, overweight woman was waving at me, but where was Anna?

"Rachel, I was just about to call you," a familiar voice shrieked. "And here you are! We both got here at the same time! You look amazing."

Never comfortable with fake compliments and feeling my bladder's urgent call, I managed a short greeting.

"I have to pee so bad, can we find a restroom first?"

"I know, it's almost like when we were raising our kids, except now it's us who are staking out the restrooms," Anna said.

"Hey, we are not clipping diaper coupons yet," I laughed.

"Only for the grandchildren," Anna said.

"Right," I said.

Ryan, my son, was a senior in high school but often reminded me of a carefree kindergartener, slurping Cheerios and still wearing his favorite oversized T-shirt from Little League. It would be a long time before I was showing baby pictures to my friends.

"Just wait till you have grandchildren," Anna said. "It's the best. I get to babysit three days a week. I am exhausted when they leave but can't wait for them to come back."

I imagined a mini version of my son showing up on a Monday morning to be left in my care while Ryan dashed off to earn a respectable living. Ryan in a suit and his worn-out sneakers was too funny. I laughed out loud.

"What's so amusing?" Anna asked.

"Picturing Ryan as an adult when he can barely manage to put his clothes in the hamper."

"It goes fast," Anna said. "First they graduate from high school, then college, then you walk them down the aisle."

I wouldn't know anything about that, I thought. It wasn't like you invited me to celebrate any of these milestones.

"Plus, I don't think my boss would be too happy if I didn't show up for work so I could babysit my grandchildren." That didn't come out the way I had intended.

"But don't you still own your own practice?" Anna frowned, adding even more wrinkles to her leathery forehead.

"Exactly." I smiled. "Let's get some lunch; I am starving. You picked this place, so lead the way."

The small, touristy Amish shopping mall had a colorful collection of quilt stores, souvenir places and restaurants with peculiar-sounding names. Oddly, a store with cowboy hats and boots, and Native American jewelry was among the mix.

"Can we go in real quick?" I asked, admiring a pair of boots in the window.

"Sure, but it's really expensive," Anna hesitated.

"It will only take a minute," I said.

"I love your dress," the young saleswoman said. "Did you get it at Forever 21?"

"Thanks," I smiled. They don't sell Stella McCartney at Forever 21.

"You know, I don't remember. Could I try on the black boots from the window in an 8?"

"Oh, I love those," she gushed. "Just a minute."

Anna looked around, picking up a pair of moccasins, then quickly put them back on the display shelf.

The saleswoman returned with the boots. I quickly tried them on and walked around to check out the fit. They were perfect. I saw Anna staring at my boots.

While I paid, Anna stood beside me, shifting awkwardly.

"Ready for lunch?" she asked, walking slightly ahead of me as we left the store.

Within minutes we were seated at a place bragging about pork, sauerkraut and pretzels. We busied ourselves with menus, napkins and what to order. After the server left, an uncomfortable silence set in, like a room that had been empty for a long time.

"So," I said. "What's going on? How are you?"

"Everything is great. Don is still working. I don't think he will ever retire. The kids all have good jobs."

A detailed description of Anna's three children embellished by photos of toothless grandchildren accompanied our meal.

"And when you don't babysit, what do you do?" I asked.

"The week goes by so fast, sometimes I wonder myself. I try to volunteer as much as I can at the Senior Center."

"What do you do there?"

"Mostly just help serve meals, chat with the residents."

This is why you went to law school? Worked your ass off for three long years? So you can freaking chat with old people? Who was I kidding, meeting Anna had been a huge mistake.

"And what about you?" Anna asked. "How is Martin? Does he still like being a judge?"

Really, I just won a national award for my pro bono work and you ask about my husband? Oh, that's right, you wouldn't even know about that.

I talked about Martin's job and our son's laid-back attitude toward school. I even threw in a funny story about Connor, the cat.

We both ordered coffee, having covered our respective families.

"You really look great." Anna said, sipping her coffee. "You haven't gained a pound, have you?"

"More than one," I laughed. "Trust me, getting up at 5 every morning to work out is not my favorite thing to do. Remember how we used to pull all-nighters eating junk food? I don't even remember what French fries taste like."

We both laughed.

"I sneak in small fries with happy meals all the time. I tried Zumba but it's hard with the babysitting."

Try getting up at 5 in the morning, I thought, not liking myself at all.

"Your children must be so grateful," I said. "To have a babysitter who can jump in at any time. God, I remember how hard it was to take care of Ryan when I first started my own practice. He had ear infection after ear infection, strep throat, constant colds. Martin and I would fight over whose turn it was when day care called to pick him up. The guilt alone. Was I doing enough for my child? Did I shortchange my clients? That was tough. Your kids are very lucky."

"I can't imagine leaving my children with strangers, especially if they are sick."

"Well, it's not exactly a choice," I said, looking straight at her.

Anna looked away.

"I am just happy to be near my children. We all live within minutes of each other. There is always something going on. I am always busy."

"I guess busy is good?" I asked. Today was the first full day off I had in months.

"You should see my house around the holidays. People and stuff everywhere. A lot of times I can't wait till the last person leaves."

"But are you happy?" I asked.

Instead of answering my question, Anna pulled out her phone to show more pictures. I looked at photos of people admiring Thanksgiving turkeys and lining up Christmas pies.

Our coffees had been refilled twice. The server had already asked once if we needed anything else, then placed the check strategically in between us.

"Oh, let me get this." Anna quickly picked up the bill.

"No way," I said, grabbing the piece of paper and fumbling for my wallet.

"Only if you promise to let me pay next time," Anna said, sitting up straight.

Next time? Would there be a next time? Time surely had not been a gift.

"Sure," I said. "Let's go. I want to beat rush hour traffic."

✝

Bright Ringing
Suzanne Grieco Mattaboni

S ometimes I talk to people I thought were gone, and they answer.

My bedroom was scattered with mementos from the day camp where I was a junior counselor, right before my sophomore year of high school. A scallop shell from a beach party. Bottle caps from after-hours camp softball games. A leather hippie bracelet with my name stamped on it from Art & Crafts class. My favorite was a little brass bell, with a stem and a hole in it for stringing.

Me and my counselor buddies, Jenna and Kate, took a shine to the bells, so we each brought one home from Arts and Crafts. I strung mine with thread and hung it on a shelving unit next to my bed.

Jenna and I had been camp buddies since we were 12, but Kate was one of my new best friends. We'd steal away on camp breaks for long conversations about boys, over-protective parents, and the general idiocy that was high school. After camp ended, we stayed in touch with each other's lives via phone. Her hair was finally growing. She liked this new guy.

On a beautiful, ordinary spring day, Jenna called me. She just heard Kate had been hit by a car walking home from a friend's house.

Kate died.

I held the phone to my ear and slid down my dining room wall. I asked Jenna why she would lie to me. None of my friends ever died. We were indestructible.

I cried to Jenna. I cried to my mother. I cried to my favorite aunt, who worked at Kate's high school.

All the junior counselors made plans to attend Kate's services, but my father insisted I wasn't allowed to go. 'Too traumatizing,' he said, and refused to drive me. I was adamant. I ranted. How could I not be there for her?

Dad took me aside. "You don't want to go to that funeral, Angela."

"What are you talking about?"

"You don't understand," he explained. "Kate is Jewish. Jewish families don't like to make a big emotional fuss when someone dies. They're not going to want a little Italian girl there, crying her eyes out."

They're not going to want me there? My heart crumpled like a recycled tin can.

All the other junior counselors went.

My friends who could drive offered me rides, but my father insisted I not go. By that point I was afraid to show my face anyway, drama queen that I supposedly was. The last thing I wanted was to make things more difficult for Kate's family. I settled instead for running across my front lawn and screaming into thin air under our pine tree.

I sat up late in my bedroom that night, and hand-wrote a letter to Kate's parents, explaining what a good friend she was. Not everybody knew how to be a good friend, but Kate did. I apologized for not being able to attend the memorial service. I told them all I could do to make sense of it was to think that God sometimes has to take good people so that they can stand as examples for the rest of us, remind us how precious life is, and to teach us to live better lives. I wanted to believe the people we love never truly leave us, even when they die, and that Kate will always be with the people who love her.

Drops of mascara decorated the pages as I wrote. I smeared them away with the flat of my fist and addressed the envelope. *Please let this be the right thing do to, God,* I thought. *I don't know a lot about this stuff.*

Whatever cultural inconsistencies supposedly existed between our two religions, I didn't understand them. I only hoped they could be transcended. That, and by sending my correspondence, I hoped somehow her parents would gain even an inkling appreciation of how much Kate meant to friends like me.

I woke up. It was a moonless night. I could barely see the outline of the mini-blinds on my window.

I sobbed. My friend was gone.

Unbelievable.

I'm sorry I missed your service, I thought. *I wish you knew how wounded I feel knowing you're gone. I want to know you're still out there, and still my friend. I hope my letter to your parents helped instead of hurt. I didn't get to say good-bye. I'm so mad. I still don't get it.*

I wanted to just talk to her, like we once did every day, splayed out on filthy gymnastics mats at camp, staring up at the sun through a screen of swaying pine boughs. Or at the picnic tables on the paint-peeled porch where the junior counselors used to gather for breaks.

I bawled like a kindergartner in the dark. My sinuses swelled like a sponge. I blindly whipped my arm toward my shelves and yanked a tissue from a box I knew was sitting there.

BRING-a-bing-ding-bling-bring-ding-a-bing . . .

I froze. In the blackness, the bell rang. LOUDLY.

I couldn't see so much as a shadow. But I knew that piece of copper was bouncing at the end of its thread like a jack rabbit. The sound reverberated in the dark.

Kate's bell.

For weeks after, I'd walk past my bed and flick the tiny brass bell, the one I knew she had owned as well. I called it *Kate's bell*. I listened to its high-pitched trill as it popped up and down on its string and said, "Hi, Kate," each time it rang.

I believe the world is a much less complicated place than people make it out to be.

Sometimes we talk to people we thought were gone, and they answer. Maybe it happens when your world is at its darkest, and you're alone, when it's quiet enough for you to actually hear them.

Clear as a bell.

For Ilene Silverman, 1980

✝

The Smile
Jerome W. McFadden

We never made a great distinction between boys' and girls' sports at Johnson County High School. We rarely had enough students to fill any of the teams. If we were short on a few slots for field hockey, we'd draft a couple of skinny freshman boys and tell them not to cut their hair for the rest of the season. Conversely, girls were welcome to try out for any team they wanted, as long as they promised not to cry if they got hurt. And, of course, for the past four years we had Margaret.

Margaret was the standout on our football team, on both defense and offense, the star of our basketball team, and the mainstay on both our baseball and track teams in the spring, when their schedules did not conflict. Which never happened, until last year, on a fine Saturday afternoon in April, when the baseball team had a home game, and the track team hosted a dual meet with the same school, just across the road. Both sides agreed that Margaret could pitch the game, and compete on the track when it wasn't her turn to bat.

It started out well. In the first inning of the ball game she hit a home run, trotted around all three bases to touch home, then jogged across the road to the track without stopping, to sprint down the runway to win the long jump on her first try.

An official from Mesquite High protested that it was not right to have someone competing on the track in a baseball uniform, wearing cleats. I argued that it would be worse to have a girl on the baseball field pitching in running shorts, a singlet, and track shoes.

We had a heated debate but reached a compromise. A small tent (it looked more like a teepee) was set up next to the track to allow Margaret to make a quick change from baseball into track clothes, and then quickly return to baseball gear, as she raced back and forth across the road. Unfortunately, the winds in west Texas never really die down, and the damn tent blew away in a heavy gust just as she was changing into her running shorts. Everybody on the track stopped to watch her change. So did everybody at the baseball game.

None of this bothered Margaret. She was raised with seven brothers. If any of them stared at her too long, she'd bust them in the mouth. So she looked around, surprised to see everyone gawking at her, and then glared. Activity on both sides of the road went back to normal.

The trouble came in the seventh inning while Margaret was pitching. A beat up, old, pick-up truck pulled into the parking lot of the baseball field and a student from Mesquite scrambled out of the cab to hurry into their dugout. Their coach called for time out so the kid could change clothes and be substituted into the game. I didn't protest as I assumed that Mesquite probably had trouble getting enough players to fill their teams, just as we did, and the youngster was probably coming to the game after doing chores at home.

He was a tall, good-looking kid. Broad shoulders, straw blond hair, a slim waist, and a killer smile. He smiled coming out of the dugout. He smiled tapping the dirt off his cleats while he waited for his turn in the batter's circle. And he smiled at Margaret when he finally stepped up to the plate. She frowned at him and went into her windup. He smiled even wider and took one hand off his bat to blow a kiss at her.

The pitch went so wide that the catcher had to lunge far out to the right to bring it in, falling flat on his face. The Mesquite dugout hooted and laughed their heads off. The boy tapped his cleats again, smiling back at Margaret as if he and she were in this together, sharing a great prank.

Margaret went into her windup once again but was so flustered she bounced the ball on the ground six feet in front of home plate and the umpire shouted, "Ball two!"

She walked down to pick up the ball and turned back to the mound, but the ball fumbled out of her fingers. Fortunately, her back was turned to the umpire so she was saved from the embarrassment of him yelling, "Ball three!"

I signaled for a time out. Our catcher and third baseman joined me for a conference on the pitcher's mound. "Make him stop smiling," Margaret said to me.

"I can't make him stop smiling," I said. "It's legal to smile in baseball."

"You got chew?" she asked Bobby Ray, our third baseman. He looked sheepishly at me, knowing I did not approve of our players chewing tobacco. But he pulled a plug out of his back pocket and handed it to Margaret. She took a large bite and wadded it up into her left cheek. She chewed for a long moment before spitting the whole mess into the grass, offended.

"That shit is awful."

"Watch your language," I warned.

"You asked for it!" Bobby Ray shot back at Margaret

"Don't get smart with me, Bobby Ray, or I'll kick your ass," she threatened.

"Watch your language," I repeated.

The umpire lumbered out to join us. "You people planning to finish this game or just want to stand around for the rest of the afternoon spitting and gabbing?"

"Make him quit smiling."

The umpire gave Margaret a blank look. "What are you talking about?"

Margaret pointed at the batter. "Make him quit smiling."

The umpire glanced over his shoulder at the boy, who smiled back at him. "Maybe he likes to smile. Nothing wrong with that. Maybe he enjoys playing baseball. Nothing wrong with that, either."

"I can't concentrate with him smiling at me."

The umpire shrugged. "That's your problem." He turned away from us with a wave of his arm, yelling, "Play ball!"

"Stay focused. That's all you have to do. Just stay focused," I said. "Can you do that?"

Margaret nodded, but with an obvious lack of conviction. We all returned to our positions.

She started her windup. The boy smiled. She stopped and stepped off the mound to collect herself. "What's your name," he yelled out to her. Margaret fumbled the ball again. She bent over to pick it up but did a klutz kick all the way to second base.

I called another time out. The umpired groaned but allowed it.

"Do you want me to pull you? Little Tommie Sooner can take over out here."

"No," Margaret mumbled.

"Then throw a bean ball. Dust him off. Make him take a step back. That'll take the smile off his face."

Margaret blinked. "I can't do that. I might hurt him."

"It'll stop him from smiling at you."

I walked back to the dugout. She did as she was told. The sizzling pitch went straight at the boy's head. He ducked away at the last second, and tripping backwards, he fell flat on his back, his batting helmet spinning away.

The umpire yelled. "Ball three."

The boy got up, dusted himself off, collected his helmet, and shouted out to Margaret, "Nicely done. That was a good one." He smiled at her as if he really admired the way she had tried to bean him.

Margaret walked away from the pitcher's mound, coming over to the dugout. She flipped the ball to little Tommie Sooner without a word. He hurried out to take her place.

"Why?" I asked.

Margaret mumbled something towards the ground.

"What did you say?"

"He's beautiful."

"He's beautiful?"

"He has a beautiful smile."

We heard the honk of a bat hitting a baseball and I looked out to see the ball sailing high toward the outfield. The boy with the beautiful smile streaked around the bases. And scored. The throw to home came seconds later.

"Tommie Sooner couldn't handle him, either," I observed.

"I'm gonna take a shower and change clothes," Margaret replied. She left the dugout without looking back.

The game slowly drew to an end. Mesquite beat us by one run, thanks to their late arrival. I didn't think much about it. Just another game. There would be others. We would win some, lose some more. No big deal. I collected the bases and carried them over to the storage locker. I straightened up the dugouts, locked the gates, and came off the field, surprised to see Margaret talking to the boy beside his battered pick-up truck. She was holding herself bashfully, leaning against the truck, both arms folded across her gym bag, a timid smile on her face.

✝

Nina's Rescue
Susan Kling Monroe

It seems like such a long time ago now, and such a small thing, but left such a lasting impact on my heart.

I knew when I looked into my child's round face filled with hope and trepidation, that I was going to regret giving in. I gave in anyway. Because tucked carefully into those dainty, cupped hands was a small bird, more gray fluff than feathers streaked with black and brown and white, a faded orange on the belly. When I did not immediately answer, Nina's lower lip slid slowly out, just a bit, then began to tremble. She was so little back then. Well, not tiny, but young. And her enthusiasm knew no bounds.

"Nina, honey, you don't know how to take care of baby birds. Neither do I," I said, my voice not as soothing and authoritatively adult as I wanted it to be. The last thing I needed was to take in this stray.

"Mama," she piped back, "you always say we can find the answer. If we just look for it, we can find anything!"

My sigh in reply was heavy. "There's knowing, and there's doing. I don't have time for us to drive over to Spruce Valley, honey. The repairman is supposed to be here sometime this afternoon. Your friend there." Was that too friendly toward the unexpected intruder? I waved a hand at the bird, and said, "It needs someone to look after it who knows what they're doing." Spruce Valley was the closest animal rehab place, an hour drive from our house.

And because I can not leave well enough alone, I added, "You should have left it where you found it. Now that you've picked it up we can't put it back where it belongs." It was a measure of how much a sucker I am that I did not fuss about the grass stains on her blue denim covered knees.

"I couldn't," Nina told me, "because it was back under the yew bush. The cats got to the nest. This is the only one left." There were twigs caught in her brown hair, and a scratch on one cheek. She'd climbed up to the nest to look.

"When did the cats get outside?" I did a quick visual check that found our twin tabbies, Tigger and Hugger, slouching on the front windowsill, their furry tails leaned against the smudgy glass.

Nina gave me the look. It was that of a monarch reprimanding her fool. She'd mastered this at a young age. "Not our cats. The wild ones."

The feral population in the neighborhood had been growing. The Wilsons down the street, who did not like cats to begin with, had raged at the Home Owners Association meeting about the one that had crawled under their house to die in the middle of May's heat wave. They'd had to pay over a hundred dollars to one of the local pest control companies to remove the body, and mitigate the smell. There was a veritable plague of cats taking over the neighborhood. Someone in the vicinity was feeding them, drawing them here, and we'd seen their lean slinking shadows outside at night, taunting our indoor tigers, and leaving scat in the flowerbeds.

"If I put him back outside where I found him, that will be like feeding the wild cats, and that's not allowed," Nina told me seriously, as she still held the baby bird out to me.

"Alright." It took all of my strength not to sigh again. "Go and find a shoebox, and then we can get his nest. We'll do some research and find out what we need to do to take care of him."

Then, when she settled the fledgling into my hand with exaggerated care, I told her, "We'll look up what it says online. But we're only watching him until we have time to get to Spruce Valley. Only until then. Right, Nina?"

She gave a quick nod in reply, but didn't look back at me. Of course, she dumped my white pumps onto the bedroom floor instead of looking for an empty box. All of her shoeboxes were being used—filled with tiny plastic dolls and animals. Trailing behind me, down the front steps and across green grass wet from the sprinklers, Nina swept her arm out like a game show hostess. "See?"

The nest was empty, which I'd expected. An adult robin, and several of our baby's siblings lay scattered under the bush, headless and forlorn corpses just beginning to attract the legion of ants that lived in our soil. *I'll need the shovel,* was my first thought. Typical. Humanity's immediate reaction to a mess is to organize cleanup.

Nina put a sneakered foot onto a limb of the arbor vitae to hoist herself up to the nest hidden behind the spiky green foliage. The bowl of woven twigs parted from the higher branch easily, it was tightly built, didn't come to pieces in her fingers, and my girl had soon tucked it into the gray cardboard walls of the shoebox. I delivered the bird into her careful hands, and she cooed over it as she placed it carefully into the center of the nest. It didn't stay. It hopped out of the nest and scrabbled about on the cardboard floor of its prison. Was it searching for an escape route?

"Set it up on the back porch," I directed my darling nuisance, "High enough so that the cats won't get it. Make sure it's in the shade." I knew where the shovel was. In the shed. Somewhere.

When I got back, after pulling apart the garden shed, Nina had already picked up the dead bodies and tossed them into the woods nearby. "You are going to wash those hands thoroughly with a ton of soap before you touch anything else," I told her. "And you get to put the shovel away after you situate your bird friend."

Nina was so excited over the bird that she didn't complain, not even when I made her wash a second time. This time with antibacterial soap (which we do not usually use, and so I had to search it out from underneath the sink), and far more extensively than her first try at briskly running fingers under the tap. She carried her iPad out to the back porch and did her research from there. "To keep him company," she said.

There was nothing for it but to bring my own laptop out. We sat on the porch in the sunshine, enjoying the summer breeze in our hair, and sipping cold glasses of lemonade, as we looked for details on how to take care of baby birds. There are a lot of sites out there. Most of them warn about removing animals from their habitat. That ship had sailed, unless we wanted to put the bird out as a snack for the midnight cats.

"It's illegal?" Nina's eyes were round as I read that bit of information.

"Illegal to raise wildlife in your home. Unless you get a permit," I agreed.

"But why?" came with a furtive glance toward the shoebox and its occupant, who had calmed down somewhat, and was sitting squashed under the edge of the nest. Otherwise the box was Spartan. We had read online that it was bad to force the bird to eat if we didn't know what it naturally fed upon. One day was not going to starve it. "He won't die of thirst, will he?" she asked.

I had no idea. "I guess it won't drown if you put a little cup of water in there," I started, but hadn't finished before Nina had put water in one of my good quarter cup measures and brought it back outside. "Oh, honey," I whined. But really, what difference did it make? I was going to wash the measure afterward anyway.

We never did see the bird drinking from its water bowl, in any case. Though I did find him sitting in it later. When I came out to check on the thing. And to take pictures. Because Nina decided that we'd document our treatment of the rescue victim with her iPad. And because I had to get out of the kitchen. Staring at the repairman, who had finally shown up, was not making him move any more quickly.

When John got home from work that night he was greeted with a kiss and a, "We've got a guest," before Nina jumped into his arms for her hug.

"Daddy," she sputtered in her driving need to be the first to tell him all that had occurred, "I found a baby bird today. And he's out on the back porch in a shoe box. And we're taking him to Spruce Valley tomorrow."

Nina absolutely had to give her father a tour of sites associated with the incident, and the full description of the morning's events. She insisted on introducing him to our guest as well. She never did give it a name, and thank heavens for that. They were on the back porch for some time, while I banged pots and pans and generally threw together dinner. Over supper

John said, "I put some weighted mesh over top of the shoe box. It seemed friendlier than putting the lid on top with some holes punched in it. Lets more air in, anyway.

"And I put our guest on the mantelpiece so that the cats won't get him during the night." The light glinting on his glasses lens made his sideways smile more naughty. Great. It was now two against one.

"Do you think he'll be bored?" Nina asked. Nina's boredom usually required application of Disney movies.

"It will be fine," I told her dismissively before realizing how much I sounded like my grandmother. No, better not do that. Trying again, I said, "Birds are not like people, honey. They might get bored, but that little bird has had as much excitement today as it needs for a long time. It will be fine."

John agreed. Then added, "Of course, we could read in the study until bedtime. Then at least he'll have some company, and a little bit of noise."

Nina picked *Cockatoos*, along with a mile high stack of other stories, and she and her father took turns reading out loud until bedtime. I tried to immerse myself in a library mystery, but gave that up to lie back on the sofa and listen to the pair of them, their reading punctuated by attempts at acting out the voices of the bird-related characters.

I'd like to say that the visit to Spruce Valley went well, and that Nina's bird lived happily ever after. The thing is, we don't know. We delivered the bird, in its cardboard container—nest and all—to the rehabilitator there. The tall, weathered-looking woman met us in the driveway and was not impressed with our little girl and her shoebox. She remembered us bringing in a cat-bitten young rabbit two years before. We've kept Tigger and Hugger inside ever since, but that scored us no gold stars in her eyes.

The rehabilitator looked into the box, "Fledgling," she sniffed. "You should have left it where it was. The parents would have looked after it."

There was much explanation, both on my part and Nina's about the dead parent birds, the other ripped up baby birds, the neighborhood's feral cat problem, to no avail. Giving a horse-like snort, the rehabilitator told us, "I'll take care of it." Carrying the shoebox, she stepped back into her office

60

and closed the door solidly behind her.

"Oh," Nina said, her voice small, quiet. Then, "I wanted to look around."

"Honey," I told her, "I think we've been given the sign to clear off."

"Oh," she responded, "okay."

The drive home was unnaturally quiet. Quiet is not Nina's, nor my, typical behavior. Nina watched out the window while the radio played Sousa marches, unheard by either of us. We did try to call the rehabilitator. We left messages checking for updates, asking if the bird had survived.

"Most robins die in their first year, but they can live to be five or six," Nina wrote in an illustrated story about the bird growing up and building his own nest in an arbor vitae. I took photographs of Nina sitting on the back porch, her tongue tip poking out of the corner of her mouth as she concentrates on what comes next in the pile of papers and crayons on the table before her.

I still have them—the story and the photographs of the bird and the picture of Nina writing. Nina used the photos in a class project in third grade, but I kept copies in a folder labeled "the bird." The story, told in crayon on plain copy paper, is smudged, but still legible.

In middle school Nina went to a local environmental camp. There's a regional newspaper with photographs of Nina helping with a Conservancy bird banding. And in high school she worked with a community college class to net bats for a study. I have photographs of her for that, smiling and intense.

No, I'm not a hoarder. I was clearing out the filing cabinet when Nina graduated from college. For a time I thought Nina would be a writer, based on that little flurry of storytelling. One likes to think that one can predict the future for children. My baby—even as an adult she's still my baby—has different ideas.

John and I got a call last night from her zoo, on the other side of the country. Shoveling manure, to be sure, and cleaning cages, but also feeding the birds, and learning everything she can to round out her bachelor's in zoology. It's a tiny place, but it's a one more step. After that, hard work as an apprentice learning to handle raptors. Then joining a research team. Someday she'll be working as a rehabilitator herself, permit and all. Nina has big plans.

And the last piece of paper in that file is a cheerful card of a robin pulling out a worm. Outside, in Nina's scratchy handwriting, it says, "Mom and Dad." Folded inside is a printout, a page off the internet that reads, "As of February, 2001, the longest-living banded wild robin ever recorded had survived 13 years and 11 months, according to the Bird Banding Laboratory at the Patuxent Wildlife Research Center. In captivity, robins have survived longer than 17 years. Ornithologist Jane Erickson."

Someday, when a little girl or boy appears on her doorstep with a shoebox in their hand, and a story of rescue on their lips, I don't think that door will be shut. And I know that she will draw that child in to the work of conservation. I'm glad, now, that, unlike that first rehabilitator, I did not shut the door on Nina's first rescue.

✝

Bill, I Love You So
Florence Morton

The gray skies and chilling drizzle of a dreary early December day in 1957 shrouded us as we relocated from West Chester County in New York to a small north Jersey town. Inside the split level house not even the combination of bright yellow walls of the living room, or the coral paint of the dining room, so small our furniture barely fit in it, nor the turquoise color of the tiny kitchen could brighten this transition.

Dad didn't like the layout of the house. "Too hard to heat in winter," he said, but offered some light when he added, "We'll rent it for a year and look for a home and area that we like better."

Without delay, Mom enrolled me in the Catholic school. The principal, a petite nun, who looked to me to be about 90 years old, displayed kindness towards my mother and me when Mom asked if I would need to buy a new uniform to match the school's green one. The one I had was burgundy.

"For just six more months of school she can wear the uniform she has," the principal said. I understood the decision, but squirmed at the thought of standing out in my odd colored uniform.

The eighth grade nun, an obese woman, was a tyrant. Each day she listed assignments for each subject on the chalkboard and directed us to write it down in our copybooks. While we wrote, the nun sat at her desk sorting out the milk tickets. Mid-morning she directed a student to sell candy, a fundraiser for the school. Just before lunch she asked several boys to take the milk tickets to the kitchen, count out the milk and deliver it to each class.

It was pretty easy, also very boring. But it gave us kids an opportunity to be creative. When the nun wasn't looking, we passed notes about "who in the class liked who." We'd hide the note inside a pen or pencil, or pass it with an eraser.

"Bring that to me," the nun demanded one day when she intercepted a note I wrote. Embarrassed, I slid down in my seat as far as I could without falling off. My face burned red-hot as she read aloud to the class what I had written to Mark, a boy I had a crush on. She said no more but continued to glare at me with her rosy pudgy-cheeked face, all you could see of it, the rest wrapped in white linen. At lunch time when I tried to leave the room the nun blocked the doorway with her large body.

"Excuse me, Sister," I said trying to squeeze past her. She pushed against my shoulder to stop me.

"You with special privilege in your burgundy colored uniform think you're better than the rest of us, you get special exception not to wear green like the rest of the girls, and writing notes to boys in class. Your mind surely isn't on school work. I think I'll just notify the principal of Holy Family Academy where you're planning on going next year and tell her to take your name off the list. I'm sure she doesn't want girls like you in her school." When she stopped her tirade I left the classroom and went home for lunch. Mom, so astounded when she heard my story, didn't even comment on my note writing transgression.

Although I didn't hear the conversation Mom said later that day that she "minced no words" when she spoke with the principal during that afternoon. The incident ended with no further comments from the nun. I passed the entrance exam and enrolled for Holy Family Academy, looking forward to a new environment where I would be dressed the same as the other girls.

During that summer the teenage kids on our block gathered at Joanne and Johnny's house, our neighbors, on Friday night for a pizza party. I hadn't tasted pizza before this, but soon it became a regular menu item in our house. At one of our Friday night parties, a boy named Bill, a friend of Johnny's joined the group.

Bill lived three blocks away, and delivered newspapers on our street. His strawberry blonde wavy hair, green eyes, and robust build were eye stoppers.

He sure stopped mine. One summer day, I watched as he rode his bike down our street after completing his deliveries. Bill liked Betty who lived a few doors down from me. As I watched him stop in her driveway, get off his bike and go to her door my heart yearned for it to be my door. Lucky for me Betty didn't respond to Bill's overtures so I took advantage of the opportunity. I was sure to be at Joanne and Johnny's pizza parties every Friday and made sure to sit next to him so we could talk.

"How old are you?" I asked.

"I'll be sixteen on my next birthday. How old are you?"

"I'm thirteen. When's your birthday?"

"It's October first, you know the day that all the *bills* come in," he chuckled at his own joke. "No really, my mother says that's how I was named Bill." I laughed. By the end of the summer Bill and I had become friends.

One day before the new school year started, we rode our bikes to his house. A shrine to the Blessed Mother graced the front garden. "It's my mother's," Bill explained, "She has great devotion to the Blessed Virgin Mary. She wants Mary to guide her to be a good mother." Bill introduced me next to his father who looked at me and said, "Hey, Billy. Robbing the cradle, aren't you?"

Though Bill was a few years older, I didn't care. I had someone with whom I could share feelings and thoughts, someone who was warm, gentle. I could talk about anything and Bill would listen. There was no condescension. There was no bullying, no arguing or discord. I felt accepted, happy, and content.

Bill attended the local public high school. I commuted on a twenty minute train ride to my all-girls Catholic high school. He gave me his ring to wear, but I kept it a secret, feeling that my parents wouldn't approve of our "going steady" status. Bill and I talked on the phone every night. I guess I spent too much time talking and not studying because when first quarter report cards came out in the fall, I failed World History. I'd never failed anything before in school and I was humiliated and worried about what Dad would say.

"You're grounded until your next report card," Dad scolded when he reviewed the card.

That meant until January, after all the holiday events were over. No football game with Bill at his high school, no Christmas parties. What awful timing.

Thankfully when Thanksgiving came, Dad relented and let me go to the football game with Bill. He even let me accept Bill's invitation at Christmas time to go to Radio City Music Hall to see the holiday show, when Bill's mother offered to chaperone.

Though school kept us apart, Bill and I found a way to meet any day we wanted. After the holidays we implemented that plan. Each morning he would leave his home early and stop to see me before continuing on with his deliveries. He came in through the lower level back door of my house into the recreation room where we wouldn't disturb anyone else in the house. I didn't mind at all getting up at 5AM to spend those few minutes with Bill before leaving for school. It was fun to start my day with him.

Our plan worked well. We met in the shadows of pre-dawn and soft lighting from the kitchen a short flight of steps away. We whispered, laughing at the success of our creativity, talking about anything and everything, enjoying our friendship. One late January morning, the same day that I would be taking the World History mid-term exam, Bill pulled a chair over, sat down, and pulling me gently guided me to his lap. His arms swaddling me, he looked deep into my eyes. His face moved closer to mine when suddenly a soft shuffling sound chilled the moment. Startled, we peered through the darkness at the outer door to see a figure standing in the threshold. My already-pounding heart beat faster. The body moved closer and the intruder's identity became clear. It was Bill's mother.

"Ah. So this is what you've been up to leaving the house so early each day," she said to her son. "Did you really think I wouldn't hear you going out the door? Haven't I told you before," she continued haughtily, "I can hear the *grass grow*!"

Eyeing the two of us, "You two are to see the priest, today! And to be sure you get there, I will take you! Now you, sir, go finish your paper route!"

she stated scornfully. She headed to the doorway pushing Bill in front of her. She stopped and turned to me, "You, Miss, can call me to let me know what time you'll be home from school."

How no one upstairs heard what was happening below them I'll never know.

About an hour or so later I frantically phoned Bill's mother from the station while waiting for the train. "I'm sorry," I said in an attempt to apologize. Deep down I wasn't really sure for what. I wasn't sorry for enjoying a moment with my special friend or for loving someone who happened to be her son, or for wanting to be loved back.

"Do you want to tell your parents or shall I tell them?" Bill's mother asked straightforwardly.

"I'll tell them," I answered back just as straightforwardly.

"What time can you be at the rectory?" she demanded.

"I can make the call myself," I responded. I held back the anger that boiled inside me.

"No. I want to be sure that you both get there."

Since exams would end the school day early, an appointment with the parish priest would be scheduled for that afternoon. The arrival of the train ended our conversation. As I climbed the steps into the car the image of the Blessed Mother shrine in front of Bill's house came to mind and I wondered if the Blessed Mother would treat her children this way.

The World History exam was a critical one. I *had* to pass it to earn back the privileges that Daddy had taken away and regain academic success to feel confident again in school. But how could I put this morning's intruder visit and the thought of its ramifications aside and be able to concentrate, remember all those historical events, and people, and dates?

Settling as best I could in my homeroom, I watched as Sister Anne, who also taught World History, passed the examination forms to us. The test was divided into segments: matching columns, multiple choice, and fill in the blanks. As she monitored the examination, at intervals she'd walk up and down each aisle, checking each ones progress. Uneasy with her close supervision, I pushed myself to concentrate despite her watchful eye. To my surprise, the answers came easily. I matched the items in Column A to Column B, pretty sure I had them right. I continued to the multiple choice segment, completing that section without too much doubt. But I couldn't complete the last section. I was stumped. I read each sentence over and over, slowly, gradually words came to mind that seemed to fit the context, but insecurity blocked my memory.

Just write, I thought, forcing my hand to complete the facts in front of me. Still one question continued to elude me. *I think 'Egyptian' is the missing word to complete this fact, but, I'm not sure. Would it be better to leave it blank than write a word there that might not make any sense?"*

At that moment Sister Anne stopped and looked at my paper. I felt embarrassed that I wasn't finished and feared the answers I already entered were wrong. She pointed to a word in a sentence at the top of the page, "Egyptian." Then she pointed to the space I had left blank, then back to the word "Egyptian." As though not surprised by her action, I wrote "Egyptian" in the space and handed in the paper. Sister Anne's unsolicited help and kind support not only freed me to complete the test, but also gave me strength to face the afternoon.

The meeting with Father Raymond began punctually. The young, overweight, priest sat stiffly behind his desk. His dark curly hair bristled as his brown eyes stared through his thick black-rimmed glasses. I recounted the story of my tryst with Bill. His questions were brusque and matter-of-fact.

"Did he touch you?"

"No. Well, yes," I stammered. "He put his arms around me; he hugged me, kissed me."

"Is that all?"

"That's all," I said. The priest directed me to go to confession, "Say exactly what you just told me. And you and Bill are not to see one another again." How cold. How harsh. I answered frigidly, "Yes, Father."

When I told my mother what happened, she scowled, "We'll see what your father has to say about it."

When Daddy came in from work, he didn't mention it. But the next morning as he was driving me to the train he said, "Now, I just want you to remember. You're getting older. When you're with boys, you need to be careful." It was that quick. Daddy gave his advice and the incident was over.

"Okay, I will." I answered, soothed by his gentleness, secure in and warmed by his love.

I don't need right now to be in love, I thought. *I'm happy just being loved.*

Sunshine broke through the early morning clouds as I exited Daddy's car.

✝

Deadly Embrace
Christopher D. Ochs

"Rhea *Chelsea* Tomblin," rang out a voice that combined the endearing qualities of a Model T aa-oo-gah horn and a battleship klaxon. "You are snoring."

The rankling voice snapped Rhea out of herself. She pinched the bridge of her nose and rubbed the cobwebs of a trance from her eyes.

Staring at business reports during a rainy commute home was bad enough, but the ones labeled "Board of Directors Only" were filled with endless back-patting when the news was good, or packed with misdirection wrapped in obfuscation when it might put a higher-up's promotion in jeopardy. Any kernel of usable information about her company's latest hostile takeover was buried under so many layers of doublespeak that Rhea slid into a hypnotic stupor.

"Godfrey, was that you?"

"No, Madam," replied the autodriver, its formal monotone in vivid contrast to the electronic sandpaper that still scraped in her head.

"Then what was that?"

"To what do you refer, Madam?"

"Never mind," Rhea snapped back at the autodriver. Autonomous vehicles had a stellar safety track record, but their user interfaces were sterile, officious and often aggravating.

She crossed her legs, resolutely turning her attention back to the reports and analyses of the newly acquired company's prospectus. Perhaps their breakthrough AI software would improve the uninspired interface. Barely a minute had passed when she whooshed a sigh of frustration.

A nagging feeling ruined her concentration. Some nameless problem dogged at her heels—but what was it? Some task unfinished at headquarters? An incriminating document left on her CEO office desk? Had she forgotten a gift for her lover awaiting her at home? No, no and *definitely* no.

Rhea glanced at the Tiffany-blue bag on the seat next to her, and shivered with anticipation for what surprise Andrea might have in store for their six-month anniversary. If it was anything like their three-month celebration's boudoir gymnastics, she might have to take tomorrow off to recuperate.

Her gaze meandered out the rain-streaked window into the charcoal evening, and a sly grin worked its wicked way onto her face. Farm fields across the undulating hills of Virginia leisurely flowed past, dimly illuminated by distant city lights bouncing off low roiling clouds. Rhea was content to allow the pastoral scenery unwind her tension, until a hulking mill flashed past the window, its enormous waterwheel frozen under a mountain of kudzu.

Rhea collapsed her UDTV tablet, and dropped it in her suit's hip pocket. "Where are we, Godfrey? I don't recognize this road."

"Lee Highway, paralleling Interstate 81," replied the soothing voice. "An accident has closed a significant portion of the interstate. We shall arrive at Madam's residence with a half-hour delay."

Rhea snarled in mild disbelief. "Why tonight of all nights?" she mumbled with unconcealed impatience.

Accidents were rare, but not unheard of. When one did occur, it was most often caused by a network outage or two boneheaded Luddites who refused to make the switch to autonomous driving, only to smack into each other.

Rhea's jaw clenched—something was not right. "Godfrey, where are the other autodrivers?"

"Madam?"

"If there were an accident on the interstate, there'd be an entire procession of cars avoiding the traffic jam, lining this highway in both directions. Where are they?"

"I'm afraid I have no explanation, Madam."

A frequency-scrambled voice came across the speaker, chilling Rhea's blood.

"Quite observant, Rhea Chelsea Tomblin."

Then it wasn't Godfrey that woke me up.

"But then I'd expect no less from you," the grinding voice continued. "It's because there *is* no accident, of course. You're not even on Lee Highway —I directed your autodriver to take a side road off the beaten path quite a while ago."

"Godfrey!" Rhea lunged from her rear seat, ignoring the restraints that bit into her hip and shoulder. "Command override 'Tomblin Indigo.' Stop this car immediately. Alert company security and the police."

Silence followed her command, broken only by the engine's revving as the vehicle accelerated onto a long straightaway. Rhea gripped the headrest of the empty seat in front of her and leaned forward. Her shoulders slumped when she scanned the autodriver displays. The GPS showed the last vestige of the interstate and Lee Highway blipping off the map.

"Please remain calm, Ms. Tomblin. I wanted to discuss certain things with you before you reach your destination."

Even in a disguised voice, Rhea might have picked out an emotion in her hijacker—anger, sarcasm, *something* in its pacing to clue her in as to a motive. But the speaker's cadence behind the scrambler was as flat and lifeless as the electronics enshrouding it. Rhea ripped her tablet back out of her pocket, snapping it open to full size. She tapped on its surface like a woodpecker, but the device remained dark.

"If this is a kidnapping, what do you want? Money? Property?" Rhea said with venom that could dissolve steel. "Influence?"

"Nothing as vulgar as that. I have no interest in any material thing you possess or power you wield."

Rhea's typing became more frantic. She pounded the surface in frustration.

"And that will do you no good. I've blocked all other communications. It's just us—you and me."

"All right," Rhea said, allowing the restraints to reel her back into her seat. "Now that you have my full attention, what is it you wish to discuss?"

"How many people have you hurt in order to get where you are today, Ms. Tomblin?"

"Oh, God. Spare me the sanctimonious rhetoric. Get to the point."

"Humor me, Rhea. May I call you Rhea?"

She slid her useless tablet behind the Tiffany bag, crossed her legs again and folded her arms. She plastered her sternest boardroom glare on her face, posing for the good of whoever would have most assuredly hacked into the vehicle's telecomm camera. "That's a pointless question. Any executive at my level has had to inconvenience, offend, shove or even back-stab someone out of the way to get where she is today."

"Quite so. But how many individuals have you *needlessly* hurt? How many have you intentionally destroyed, just to watch the ant burn in the sun under the magnifying glass?"

"Like *you* are doing now?"

A measure of silence answered.

"Touché, Rhea. You have begun to peel away my mask. Shall I take it off completely?" A hint of teasing leaked through the snarling artificial monotone. "We are two of a kind, you and I—two sociopaths wanting what we want, when we want it. But where you lack any redeeming qualities that I am able to discern, I have learned at least one.

"She was my teacher, my single connection to the human race, the one person in all the world who brought out that sliver of innocence buried deep under the dark armor of my scarred psyche—and you saw fit to steal her away." The electronic voice became a metronome tolling a dirge. "Just because you could."

"So that's what all this is all about—an imagined romance gone sour.

And all this is some grandiose attempt at vengeance from the lover spurned." Rhea tapped her chin and rolled her eyes like a schoolgirl taunting a classmate. "Hmm . . . whose feathers have I ruffled, I wonder? Cyrus is it?" Rhea grunted with derision, and unfolded her arms to brace herself as the autodriver slowed to round a sharp curve. "You work in our IT department, do you not?"

"Please, Rhea. Do not insult our collective intelligence." The annoying growl of the scrambler switched off, replaced with a man's voice almost as bereft of emotion as its electronic avatar. "You know very well who I am. You took far too much pleasure in destroying me to feign ignorance now. You gleefully ensured that I knew who it was who usurped my software company, ruined me financially, and poisoned against me the love of whom I speak—Andrea."

"All right, Cyrus. The combatants have acknowledged each other on the field of battle. May I remind you that all is fair in love and war?"

"Love had little to do with it. Not with people as such as us—people with little or no empathy, with only id and ego to drive us, and no insufferable conscience to rein us in."

Rhea smiled a cruel half smile, inwardly reveling in the compliment paid her.

"Only some of us have more control over their baser desires than others," Cyrus continued. "It was not enough to convince Andrea that I could no longer make her happy materially. After you replaced me as CEO in my company, you then sought to replace me in Andrea's life. You wheedled at her incessantly, persuading her that what she really was looking for in a lover was you."

"Poor little man. Threatened by lesbians, are we?"

"You might hope it were that simple, Rhea. I learned long ago the alphabet soup of today's alternative lifestyles are no worse nor better than their hetero counterparts. They whimper just as sweetly, and bleed just as red. So no, your gender preference has nothing to do with it. You're simply a horrid person, Rhea.

"Stealing Andrea I could understand. I could even forgive it—surely you realize what a personal achievement that amounts to, one sociopath to another. That was how much Andrea focused me, how much she changed me. Her happiness became my happiness. An entirely new sensation, I confess, and one that I now sorely miss."

Rhea yawned and primped her hair for the benefit of her kidnapper voyeur. This was becoming as tedious as a boardroom soliloquy. Annoyed, she raised an eyebrow as the diatribe continued.

"But you were not satisfied with merely winning Andrea's heart, body and soul. You continued the assault. I'm sure you meant for me to overhear when you told her that I was 'a rigid little robot floundering in the trenches.' But a barb as small as that was insufficient for your needs. You had to utterly destroy me in her eyes to make your victory complete—to show Andrea the monster I was capable of becoming."

"Yes, the look of disgust on her face was delicious," Rhea chuckled. "But if it is not money, power, reparations or a confession you wish to extract from me, then it can only be one thing." She inhaled a solemn breath, lowered her head and gave her best death's head grin for the camera. "If you kill me, Andrea will be devastated. If you profess to be so concerned for Andrea's welfare, is that what you truly want?

"Add to that, Andrea's no dullard. She will eventually uncover what you have done, and will hate you forever for it. If you harbor some fantasy in which she will return to you, put it out of your mind. She won't."

"I came to that same conclusion." Cyrus also drew in a breath, echoing Rhea's resolve. "But I know something that Andrea doesn't—your own long line of previous romantic conquests that you have abandoned, bleeding in their tears. Whether you have hidden it from her, or she chooses blissful ignorance is of no matter. Whatever the case, I will not allow her to be harmed. You would use Andrea, take your pleasure from her, then discard her when the next trinket catches your eye. *That* would be her devastation, one I cannot permit. By taking your life now, I at least leave her with the fiction that you were a good person. A kindness you did not see fit to offer me."

A glint of oncoming headlights flashed in the distance ahead.

"And so, the knights and their steeds meet on the field of battle." Cyrus' voice held a hint of a chuckle. "It is a fitting and ironic conclusion, when you come to think of it, Rhea. In the old days of software, there was a condition referred to as a 'deadly embrace.' Two subroutines are each locked in a state, until the other one completes its task.

"In our case, each of our autodrivers is now programmed with the other's location as its destination. Shall we embrace, Ms. Tomblin?"

The headlights bounced and flashed as the approaching autodriver hurtled towards Rhea and her vehicle.

"You imbecile," Rhea snarled, her merciless anger straining to be released. "I'm already wearing my restraints, not to mention the autodrivers' half-dozen other fail-safes."

"The fifty pounds of explosive occupying the seat beside me will be more than enough to overcome them."

Rhea screamed commands at her autodriver, then fell into a dread-filled silence.

"What was it you said to your last lover, Rhea? 'Just close your eyes and hold your breath, my dear. It will hurt less that way.'"

✝

The Soldier
Bart Palamaro

The enemy has built up his forces overnight and there is pressure all along the line. It may hold, but it is up to my comrades and me to ensure that it does. I look up and down the line, each of us has a different sector to support and we are ready. We are the ones who find the weak spots and exploit them until the enemy is defeated there. Then we move on to the next fight. It's what we do to defend the line.

Behind me, the people I protect are unsuspecting, snug, warm—most of them still asleep. Not knowing the enemy is menacing them even now. If they think about me at all it is a fleeting thought, full of misunderstanding, error and confusion. And, yes, maybe some fear. But it does not matter, this is my job and I will do it to the best of my ability. My comrades and I, we stand between the defenseless and destruction. I look back to the front at the massing enemy.

It is cold. Of course it is cold, it always is. I see the next unit up the line has started attacking. I check for friendly fliers in the area. Above me in the sky, a 'V' formation is moving south. But they are well out of my line of fire. I analyze the enemy using low-level laser pulses, probing, judging, calculating his strength, discovering his flaws. When I know where the weakness is, I fire. My aim is true and my shots crack through the enemy, crashing him to the ground. I adjust aim and fire again and more fall. Again and again I fire. Working methodically, I clear the section and the line holds. Moving into the next section I see the line is under tremendous strain and it may be too much. The enemy has a heavy element here. I consider it. No, it is too formidable for me to handle alone. I need reinforcements. I contact my 'higher.' The news is not good—all along the line the enemy has brought extraordinary force to bear. I am assured that I will get help 'as soon as humanly possible.'

Well, that is the problem, isn't it?

This sector is critical; the terrain is challenging, steep and rugged. A break in the line here will be very difficult to restore, especially with the strength the enemy has shown. I ask for help from my comrades on either flank, but they cannot abandon their posts, all of them are fully engaged with merely buttressing their sectors of the line. It is up to me then, but what can I do? I have no weapons designed to deal with this. But I know that anything I can do to ease the pressure will help. Once again I probe the enemy for weakness, looking, estimating, sometimes guessing. There . . . perhaps . . . Yes! The enemy, for all his strength and mass, is precariously positioned. A properly placed attack could destroy him. I aim carefully, adjusting and readjusting until I am satisfied. I fire.

No! My attack has only caused the enemy to increase his pressure on the line. It is near the breaking point! I cannot wait for reinforcements; the situation has become critical. But the enemy has moved and is now more vulnerable than ever. I do the unprecedented. I rush forward to come to grips with the massive enemy myself. It is impossible, but I must try. It is the only option I have left, the line is near collapse and cannot hold much longer. I struggle. If I can get the leverage just right . . . I feel him giving way . . . there! Locked together, we fall and the terrain itself defeats him as he crashes to the ground and splinters apart.

Unfortunately, he has taken me with him. Things break as I hit the frozen ground. A quick self-assessment tells me this is not good. I cannot move. I send a call for help to my 'higher.' No response. I try again . . . nothing. I try to contact my flanking comrades to relay my situation, but they do not respond either. So, the radio is gone, too.

I can still observe, though. I look up and down the line as far as I can see and all along we are holding. That is good, but beyond this there is more of the enemy, and behind them, yet more. It will take a long time to defeat this attack, and the enemy will be back.

He always is.

I regret I will no longer be able to contribute to his defeat, but it is time for me to rest.

～

The helicopter clattered above the ravine. In the passenger seat, the line superintendent pointed, shouted to the pilot over his headset, "Get us lower —down there."

The pilot nodded and banked the machine towards the indicated spot. Below them in the steep, snow covered canyon, brightness and stark shadow made it difficult to see what the superintendent was pointing at. Half buried in the snow was a massive, rotten tree trunk from somewhere up the canyon wall. It had broken free in the last ice storm and come to rest here.

"This is where thirty-two-forty-three reported a downed tree on the line," the superintendent shouted.

"Well, it's not on the line now," the pilot shouted back. It had been a long day, and all he wanted was to head for the barn. Inspecting high-tension power lines along this rough stretch of country was tricky at best and downright dangerous at worst.

The superintendent grunted in reply, scanning the terrain below with binoculars. Then he spotted it. He could just make out the black lettering on the back of the construction-yellow machine where the wind had scoured the snow clear.

```
HIACHI-APLC
Autonomous Power Line
Clearing Unit # 3243
Text 5553243 to **APLSVC
To Report Malfunction
```

He nodded to himself. "OK, let's go. I've seen enough."

"Think it's worth retrieving?" the pilot asked, as he banked the chopper towards home.

"Nah, not in this country. I'll have them break one out of storage and replace it. No big deal. Let's go."

Below, only wind and wisps of blowing snow marked the soldier's grave.

✝

The Jester
Richard Rosinski

I walked toward the breakfast bar quickly. I had overslept and was late for work. The breakfast bar was at the end of the driveway. One whole wall was glass. The other walls were of aged yellow brick. I pushed open the glass door and sat down at the gray horseshoe-shaped counter that surrounded the kitchen area. I ordered breakfast and said hello to a few of the guys. Two more of the men on our crew walked in and ordered breakfast. They sat a few feet away, drinking their coffees and talking to the waitress. Jess sat at the other end of the curved bar, next to John, our boss. John was talking to the manager of the place.

"That's right, sir. We're from the electrical crew on the railroad. The company will pay for our meals. Just have each man sign his bill and the railroad will pay for them all at the end of the week."

John sat down on one of the pink stools and made a gesture to tell us all to get going. In the same moment, he picked up his coffee and chugged what was left. His face turned red, and he began to sputter and cough.

Jess turned toward him laughing and said, "Whatsa matter, Uncle John, don't you like salt in your coffee?"

"You jerk. One of these days I'll crack you in two," John spit back.

"Aw, can't you take a joke?"

John picked up a glass of water, drank it and walked out to the truck. The rest of the crew followed in twos and threes. We all wore work boots, Levi's, and dirty shirts. Half of the crew hadn't shaved in three days, and most of them bore visible signs of hangovers. Bob, who needed a haircut badly, kept brushing his long hair out of his bloodshot eyes. I kept sipping tomato juice to quiet my jittery stomach. Jess should know better than to fool around. We had all been out celebrating last night and no one had the patience to put up with his joking.

We all got into the back of a box truck that had "New York Central" painted on the side. There was a small doorway in the back. Inside, the truck was bare except for two long benches and our tool bags. We sardined ourselves in and someone slammed the door. Bob winced and grabbed his head. As the truck drove away, Jess made some remark about drinking.

All the seats along the benches were taken, so Bob stood near the door. He lurched from side to side as the truck bounced and turned. Jess jabbered about something or other while the rest of us nursed our headaches. Rocky was slumped over with his head in his hands saying, "Oh, my head."

"Yeah, but look what fun we had. Christ, I haven't been that drunk in months," someone said.

Bob shifted his weight and propped his head against the door frame. As soon as he touched it, the door flew open and he began to fall. We could see the road streaking by. He grabbed the door frame with one hand and pulled himself back in. Then he moved to the other end of the truck and leaned against the wall behind the cab. He gasped to catch his breath. I tried to shut the door, but the knob was gone.

"Alright, who's been screwing around with the door? You want to kill somebody?" I yelled.

"I didn't want anyone to get hurt," Jess said, with a grin "It was just a joke."

One of the guys swore at him and we all glared at Jess. In a few minutes, the truck came to a stop along the railroad tracks. Grabbing our tools, we hopped out. There was nothing around, except for the truck. Two tracks stretched out like twin ladders to the horizon. On both sides, the tracks were bordered by hilly cow pastures. Only the dirt road and a few rocks interrupted the scene.

Everyone formed a semi-circle around John to find out what we had to do. He assigned each man a job and then turned to me.

"Waffle, take two men and Jess and go finish up the work on that last switch. Make sure the track is clear."

Bob, Rocky, Jess and I started walking over to the switch. John called out, reminding us that the switch had ten years of dirt and grease on it and would be slippery.

I left the three men at the switch and walked over to the line phone to check with the dispatcher for clearance on the track. The phone was in a little cabinet bolted to a pole. The sides and peaked roof hadn't been painted in years. As I opened the door, white flakes of paint fell off. The phone was an old model. The letters "Press To Talk" on the call button were almost completely worn off and the earphone had a piece broken off.

I pushed the CALL button and yelled into the mouthpiece. "Hello, Tower Eight. Hello, Tower Eight."

"This is Tower Eight," a voice answered.

"Hello, Tower Eight. This is the electrical crew at CP-11. We've got some work to do on track two, switch thirty-one. Anything coming?"

"No electricians. Nothing coming on two for thirty-five minutes. Let me know when you are done."

"Okay, thanks, Tower Eight. Thirty-five minutes."

I put the phone back, closed the cabinet and yelled to the men that it was all right to start. It was getting pretty warm already. While walking back to the switch, I took off my shirt and put it on the pile with everyone else's. With a couple of wrenches I began working on one of the switches. As I bent over the switch, balancing myself on the greasy ties, I told the guys to be careful. The next thing I knew, someone grabbed my pant leg and pulled me. I fell and slid along the rails on my bare chest. A sliver of metal ripped a long gash on my chest. An oily splinter of wood drove itself into my shoulder, and grease filled the new cuts and scrapes. My head hit the rails. I looked behind me, half-dazed and heard Jess laughing.

"If you could have seen your face when you started to fall! My God, ha, ha, ha!"

I stood up and picked out Jess' shirt from the pile.

"Hey!" he yelled. "That's the only clean shirt I have."

The Write Connections

"Shut up, or I'll slug you with this wrench," I growled.

I wiped most of the grease and dirt off my skin with his shirt and tossed it back to him. Rocky ran up with some iodine, gauze pads, and tape. As he dabbed on the iodine, he asked if I wanted a doctor. I told him that I'd be all right. Jess came up and said something about me not being able to take a joke. I picked up a wrench and threw it at him. I missed his head by only six inches.

I sat down and rested until lunchtime. Then we drove back to town. We walked into a small Italian restaurant sandwiched between two tall buildings. A long bar bathed in blue light lined one wall; the other side was a row of booths. The smell of spaghetti sauce filled the air and the jukebox was spinning out *La Vie en Rose*.

We sat down at a booth at the back and ordered lasagna and beer. After a short while we were joined by the rest of the crew. The boss walked in first. He held up two fingers in a "V" as he sat down at our booth. The bartender hurried over with a bottle of Old Vienna Ale. John filled his glass and told us what had happened after we had left the job.

One of the supervisors from another department saw what had happened and had fired Jess on the spot. But John talked to the other super, said his crew was short-handed, and told him that Jess was connected to someone in management. I knew the connection was with John. So, Jess would still be working with us.

The waitress came over with our lasagna and then took John's order. I sat there eating and thinking about what happened that morning. Whenever I tried to put it out of my mind, a flash of pain seared my chest and my mind kept repeating the phrase, *Can't you take a joke? Can't you take a joke?*

Rocky and I finished our lunches, signed the checks, and walked out. Part of the crew was already outside sitting on a long row of concrete steps in front of the restaurant. I sat down and listened to the conversation. Just then, Jess came out of the restaurant and turned toward us. Everyone stopped talking and stared at him. Karl, a giant of a man, was the first to break the silence.

"Say, Jess, how does it feel to be the dumbest man on the electrical crew?"

"I don't know, Karl. How does it feel?" Jess replied.

Jess turned and walked back into the restaurant. A few minutes later, he and his uncle walked out together. John called me aside and told me to go a few miles back down the line. I was to take Jess with me and finish wiring the switches at CP-10. We should return to the motel at 4 o'clock.

Jess and I walked down the street to his car. I stopped at a little store to buy a newspaper. I knew it would be a twenty-minute drive. Reading the paper would be a reason not to talk to Jess. We got into his car, a very old, beat-up Chevy. The fenders were dented and the bottoms of the doors had rusted through. Parts of the car had been painted with primer so that it was a combination of red and green. The car floor was covered with sand and dirt. The seats were ripped. It could have been stolen from a junkyard.

When we got onto the highway, Jess started talking. "I had this car when I was in the service. I was an electrician then too, you know. We drilled a hole about two inches from the end of the exhaust pipe and fitted in a spark plug. Then we hooked it up so I could control the spark plug with a little switch under the dashboard. One day, my sergeant was following real close, so I pulled out the choke to flood the engine and fired the spark plug. You should have seen it! A big flame shot out of my exhaust and covered the sergeant's car with soot. He thought his car had blown up. It was funnier than all hell."

We drove up to CP-10 and got out of the car. There were four tracks at this point. Two were for traffic, and two had been used as freight sidings. About five feet south of the tracks was a sheer drop of thirty-five feet to the Barge Canal. On the north side was an old gray stone freight building with a slate roof. The building was at least 300 feet long with green doors spaced every twenty feet. Fronting the entire building was a rotted wooden loading platform. We walked over to the siding and stood there a second. Jess poked me and pointed to an old drunk asleep on the platform.

"Come on, let's have some fun with him," Jess said, with a nasty grin.

"No, Jess, leave the poor guy alone. Stop horsing around for once."

"Jeez, it's only a joke. Come on, let's go scare him."

"Leave him the hell alone."

I pulled Jess away and explained what we had to do. It was a particularly dangerous job. With the wind blowing the way it was, we couldn't hear a train coming. If one were to come through while we were working, we'd be goners. There was no place to jump to safety.

We went to the switch that had to be finished. I told him that I'd call the tower and make sure it was safe. As I turned and started walking to the call box, he bent down and grabbed my ankle. I went sprawling onto the gravel, landing a few inches from the edge of the drop-off to the Canal.

"You stupid fool," I yelled. I raised a fist and said, "Uncle or no uncle, I owe you one for that."

"Aw, can't you take a joke?"

I got up and walked over to the phone, my chest aching. I turned and noticed that Jess was bent over the switch. He had started working.

"Hello, Tower Seven. Hello, Tower Seven."

"Yeah, this is Tower Seven."

"Tower Seven, this is the electrical crew at CP-10. We've got some work to do on track two. Do you have any trains coming?"

"Stay off. I repeat, stay off. The express will be there any minute."

I turned around and watched the train approach Jess' hunched body. *Yeah, Jess, I can take a joke. Can you?*

✝

Amnesia Exercise: Breathing Underwater
Larry Sceurman

It is as if I woke up, not from a dream but into a dream. Sitting at the bar, with pencil in hand staring at what was scribbled on a napkin.

When the tide comes in we retreat with the backpedaling energy of fear.

When the tide goes out we advance with the frontward energy of fear.

Somewhere between the tide coming in and the tide going out,

We feel something under our feet, smooth and rough, spiny and rigid.

When we dig it up, we find that it is an ancient being.

We must learn to breathe underwater.

What is this tide coming in and tide going out, fears, ancient beings and breathing underwater? Did I write this? Who am I? Where am I? And who's this man waving a sandwich and talking at me?

"I'm telling you, there's an art to making a sandwich. Am I right or wrong? Look, you start with the bread then you put on the ham, then the cheese, then the mustard, maybe a little horseradish. With more cheese on top of the mustard, then more ham on top of the cheese, and then bread. Hey, am I right or wrong? See, everything is layered on top of each other, that's why you call it a sandwich! Is this a great sandwich or what? My crazy wife, Helen she don't know how to make a sandwich. You take peanut butter and jelly, my crazy wife puts the jelly on bread first. I tell her, 'Helen, you always put the peanut butter on the bread first, never the jelly first. A good peanut butter and jelly sandwich has peanut butter on each piece of bread and jelly in the middle.' Hey, tell me, am I right or wrong?"

The Write Connections

I'm sitting here, staring at this man with big bushy eyebrows, intense dark eyes and a big brown mustache. He's telling me how to make a sandwich. I think I might know him. At the same time, I look around, searching for clues that will bring me out of this dream. I have a wedding ring on. I must be married. And the bartender seems to know me.

The man with the mustache takes two quick bites of the sandwich, finishes his beer and puts money on the bar. Then he says to the bartender, "Sam, you got the best free lunch in town." He slaps me on the back and once more asks if he was right or wrong. He points to me and tells Sam the bartender to give Steve another drink on him and says "Good luck, we will keep you in our prayers." He salutes me and walks out.

He called me Steve. Is that my name? Steve? What is this good luck and prayers stuff? I take a sip of my beer and look down. I'm in uniform. My sleeve has two stripes, I'm a corporal. I check my pockets, there must be something in my pockets. A pack of Lucky's and a small pencil. Huh, there's also a piece of paper. I unfold it, it says, Stephen J. Kowalski. But that's my father's name, Stephen J. Kowalski. How do I know that's my father's name? I don't know who I am, how could I know who my father is? I studied the orders more carefully. I'm to report to Fort Dix, New Jersey, January 25, 1944 to be assigned to the first infantry division England.

The bartender puts another beer in front of me. I ask him about that guy with the sandwich. He laughs and says, "Your Uncle Pete was in rare form today." He wipes off the bar in front of me and sets down a coaster. A very pretty blonde woman with sparkling blue eyes sits next to me.

The bartender winks at me. "Gotta be on your best behavior now." Then he looks at the woman. "What'll you have, Ann?"

"Oh, I'll have a beer like Steve," says the blonde.

My mind swirls. I can't take my eyes off this woman. Her voice is so familiar and her eyes are haunting in a pleasant way. The bartender called her Ann.

"Steve," the blonde woman says, "I'm glad we got married before you go overseas. We only had two weeks together but it was a wonderful two weeks. I'm so happy that we honeymooned in the city. I felt funny staying at my mom's house with you." She raises her eyebrows and gives me a smile. "You know what I mean. Now it's time to get on the train. I'm not going to cry 'til I kiss you good bye."

I'm married to this beautiful woman? This is getting crazier and crazier, but better too. Then it hits me, it's her voice. I know that voice and those eyes; those big blue eyes. Her name is Ann, She's my *mom*! She's my mom before she was my mom. The guy with the sandwich was my grandfather's brother, the old guy they call Uncle Pete. Then I'm my father? But I never saw my father, my dad died in World War II. He died at Omaha Beach on D-Day. How could this be? I was born September 1944. How do I know this? I just do. I look at the orders again. They're dated, "January 25, 1944."

I look back at my mom. Look how much in love she is. Her eyes, her smile and her voice just pouring out love. Right now I'm my father and this beautiful woman is my wife. This is too bizarre . . . maybe I am breathing underwater.

†

Love Knows No Boundaries
Dawn M. Sooy

Dusk settled in the summer sky as I peered out of my mother's hospice room. The sun cast an orange and yellow glow on the tops of the city's higher buildings. Their walls of paned glass reflected the last of the bright rays like individual mirrors. The hospice allowed visitors around the clock, and Mom had asked me to spend the night with her.

Mom was eighty-three and had congestive heart failure along with kidneys that decided if the heart wasn't going to function properly, they wouldn't either. My brother had been taking care of her in his home up until the time hospice became the best choice for her care. He had called me one Wednesday morning to let me know he had admitted her to the Phoebe Home. He had started crying as he said again and again, "I just couldn't take care of her anymore. I couldn't do it." My heart went out to him, as I knew he loved Mom deeply.

"You did the best you could, Maynard. You took very good care of her. No one would blame you for placing her in hospice," and I cried along with him.

Years before Mom's admittance to the Phoebe Home, my brother and his wife, Eileen, would visit Mom at her home at least twice a week. As Mom grew older and depended more on my brother, he stepped in and took responsibility for her. I guess "responsibility" may not be the correct word, but since Mom could no longer drive, Maynard had been there to take her to the doctor, grocery store, and other places. Eventually, she'd been unable to manage the stairs in her home, so Maynard and Eileen had packed up the necessities and moved Mom into their one-story home.

Earlier that afternoon, I watched Mom take a nap in her room. When was the last time I had visited her at home? Or made a phone call to see if she needed anything? It's pretty damn sad when the answer popped into my brain and twenty years had slipped by. I hung my head and cried for all that wasted time.

A nurse's aide came into Mom's hospice room to ask her what she wanted for dinner. The nurse read the choices, and Mom replied "yes" or "no" to the selections. My brother and I both brought her strawberries on the same visit, and Mom decided she wanted me to make her a strawberry milkshake, although the suggestion came from my brother. So I mashed the fruit into little pieces and placed them into a cup of milk that I had mixed with vanilla ice cream. She took a sip and crinkled her nose. Without a blender, all she had were strawberries in milk with ice cream. She tried to drink the mixture with the straw, but the berries kept getting caught. It was disappointing, but the best part was that my Mom, my brother, and I had tried to work on something together. I asked her if she wanted me to bring her a strawberry milkshake from McDonald's or Burger King, but she just shook her head.

After my brother had left, I changed into my PJ's. Ten minutes later, a nurse wheeled in a cart with coffee, snacks, and sodas. I hugged the nurse to thank her and said, "You are so sweet to bring this in here."

There were cookies in the basket, and Mom took those. Since her heart condition limited her amount of daily liquids, she couldn't have coffee or soda. She had a cup of ice chips and was happy with them. We then settled back to watch a show on the Food Network.

When the show was halfway over, Mom mumbled, "I don't know who you are."

I turned to look at her, and her eyes were closed. Somewhere between the time the chef cooked the flank steak and prepared the sauce for the veggies, Mom drifted off to sleep. I climbed out of the recliner, brushed the hair out of her closed eyes and adjusted the nasal cannula that helped her breathe. She raised one arm and pointed at some unseen object, then dropped her arm back onto the bed. She mumbled words in her sleep that only she understood.

I whispered, "Mom, are you okay? Do you need anything?"

She opened her eyes and stared at me, trying to figure out who I was, or maybe she was still in dreamland. The way she looked at me was unsettling, as if there wasn't a person behind her eyes. A few seconds later, she closed them and continued with her ramblings. I kissed her forehead and tried not to cry.

I watched her sleep for another minute before climbing back onto the recliner and pulling the blanket up to my chin. Ever since Maynard called me, I felt the need to cram as much time with Mom and tried not to cry over the wasted months when I didn't even take the time to call her. The past is the past, and there is no way to recapture those lost moments. I try to maintain a positive outlook for the future, but somehow, the past creeps back like a fog onto the shore, obscuring the comforting glow of the lighthouse. And I cried.

I realize everyone dies, but I liked to believe Mom had lived a great life. Years ago, she won $1 million in the lottery. You know how you read the crazy stories in the newspaper about how people chose the numbers? The way Mom had picked her numbers was just as silly. She'd written all the numbers on small slips of paper and placed them on the edge of the coffee table. Her cat would then jump up and knock down some of them to the floor. That is how she had won the lottery.

In Mom's hospice room, I sat in the recliner reading and every so often, I looked up and checked on her as she slept. One time, when I looked up, she smiled at me and said, "I love you, Dawn."

Surprised by this, I replied, "I love you, too, Mom."

Our family had never been affectionate, so hearing these words and repeating them back changed our relationship. A bond formed between Mom and me, and I cherished the feeling. She smiled and closed her eyes. I sat and cried because I had been waiting years to hear those words come from her lips, without me saying them first.

Eventually, I dozed off in the night and woke to the sound of Mom calling my name. The nurse was in the room checking off what my Mom wanted for breakfast. Apparently, since I had spent the night, the nurse invited me to fill out a breakfast menu. I ordered the eggs and toast with coffee.

Mom's sudden appetite surprised me. She ordered scrambled eggs, home fries, toast with jelly, and farina. When they brought her food, she picked at some of it, but didn't eat much. The same thing happened at lunchtime. Mom ordered different items from the list, but when they brought her lunch, she just picked at the food.

Bob, my husband, had dropped me off the evening before and would pick me up sometime in the afternoon. So it seemed extra-special to spend this time with Mom. We talked about our days as partners in bowling tournaments. I had brought photos from our Connecticut and Reno, Nevada, trips. We bowled a little over our average, so we were happy even if we didn't win a prize.

Mom fell back asleep, and it was almost noon when the staff came in to change her sheets. I took a walk around the floor to give her some privacy. The coffee in the room was no longer hot, so I meandered to the cafeteria for a fresh cup. From a nearby shelf, I took a Nutra-Grain bar and a pack of shortbread cookies for Mom. By the time I walked back to the room, the bed had clean sheets. I gave Mom her cookies, and I ate the Nutri-Grain bar.

Maynard arrived in the early afternoon and teased me about getting a cart with food, drinks, and fruit. "Now I know who to talk to, to get some pull around this place."

I laughed and said, "It's just because I spent the night with her."

Bob returned to pick me up, and we stayed maybe another hour when I said, "Mom, I have to go now. I'll be back in a couple of days." I kissed her and hugged her, and before I could say it, she said, "I love you, Dawn." I hugged her tighter and said through tears, "I love you, too, Mom."

"I don't know why it was so hard to say those words before."

"I don't know either, Mom. Maybe deep down inside we knew how we felt but were afraid to speak those words out loud. At least we weren't too late to say them."

During that week, the family continued to visit Mom. On Tuesday, she became confused and didn't know where she was. She had little appetite, and spent most of Wednesday sleeping. Later that day, the dreaded phone call came from my brother.

"Dawn, Mom passed away late this evening. I have to go to Phoebe to make arrangements."

"Do you need me to do anything, Maynard?"

"Not right now. We'll get together in a few days and talk about it."

That night, while sleeping, I had a dream where Mom was standing beside my bed. She reached out and stroked my hair then said the four best words in the world, "I love you, Dawn."

✝

Unexpected Connections
Sheila Stephen

A gentle drizzle fell from the sky as Melanie Weaver made her way home from the park. She'd walked two miles and just settled onto her favorite bench with a good book. Then the drizzle began. Melanie was a busy woman who rarely took time for herself, but recently she'd found that she had to start doing exactly that. Grief had a way of opening her eyes to the voids in her life.

The local park had become a special place for Melanie. She began going there soon after her mother, Elsie, had died unexpectedly of a heart attack in Melanie's home. It had devastated Melanie to come home from work that night and find her mother at the kitchen table, head resting on her arms.

Elsie had been a healthy woman, despite some weight concerns. When she'd fallen on a cold winter morning and broken her foot, there was no possible way for her to continue living alone. Worse, Elsie had begun to show signs of senility and Melanie knew it was time to bring her mother into her home. That was two years ago, right after Melanie's divorce. She and her mother had grown closer during that time. The two had done much for each other, and now Melanie missed her mother terribly. For weeks after Elsie's death, going home felt like walking into a tomb.

This Saturday morning, Melanie had Danielle Steel's latest novel. She looked forward to sitting on the bench under the big old oak tree in the park. It was a peaceful spot that Melanie had grown to treasure. The birds sang, and occasionally a cardinal or a blue jay would make an appearance. But the drizzle began to fall steadily. While she wasn't getting wet under the protection of the oak tree, Melanie feared the rain might really pick up and she'd be soaked on make her way home. Her shoulders slumped. After a long week of challenges at work, all Melanie wanted was a Saturday devoted to some peaceful "me" time.

Damn! She couldn't even manage a few hours of quiet seclusion in the park! Lately, it felt like the whole world was picking on her. Sure, she could read at home where bad weather was of no concern. But Melanie just couldn't get past that heavy silence. It depressed her when she'd realize a creak in the floorboards was not her mom in the next room keeping busy. Elsie was gone, and home had become a lonely place.

As she made her way home, Melanie prayed silently. *"Dear God, Please stop this insanity where every little thing makes me crazy. I am way too hard on myself. I miss my mother so very much. I miss her singing "Jesus Loves Me" while she baked. I miss her meeting me at the front door at night asking me how my day went."* It only kept drizzling.

"Jesus Loves Me" was Elsie's favorite song. She'd sung it as a lullaby to Melanie when she was little. She'd sung it while she cleaned and cooked. Melanie had even heard her mother sing it with loud abandon in the shower. It had been Elsie's own personal anthem. Melanie continued her prayer, *"I miss our deep conversations about life and I miss sharing my dreams with her. I know she's with You in a wonderful beautiful place. While I am happy she's with You and at peace, I just miss her so much. Amen."*

Just then, a car blew its horn as the driver rounded the corner, splashing a puddle all over Melanie's jeans. She lost it. "What the hell!" she yelled. She knew it was only water. She took a few breaths. *Okay, calm down, the jeans can be washed.* But it sent her over the edge and tears flowed down her face. She needed to make a doctor's appointment. *If a little water sends me into a tizzy, I need some counseling!* If only her mom were here to hug her, just one more time.

Instantly and without fanfare, the rain stopped. Clouds parted and the sun suddenly emerged, revealing a brighter-than-usual rainbow at the end of the street. The fresh aroma of Mother Nature's cleansing rain was sweeter than she'd remembered. Odd, how quickly the weather had turned. One moment it was raining and the next, the sun was out!

As she passed the Church two doors away from her home, she gazed up at the steeple of the Church where a single white dove sat looking down at her. After a few seconds, the dove fluttered her wings and took off high in the sky. She caught sight of a group of children with an adult. While some of the kids were playing on the swings, most were gathered together, immersed in beams of golden sunlight. They were singing "Jesus Loves Me."

Melanie's mouth hung open in amazement. She felt joy in her heart and goosebumps on her arms. God had heard her prayer. He'd sent her not one, but *two* signs letting her know Elsie was okay. Melanie felt better now. Who wouldn't after being personally touched by God like that? She felt a connection to Him and was overwhelmed. She also felt connected to her wonderful mom.

What a beautiful day.

✝

The Visit
Emily Thompson

Alone, I am waiting on Grandmother's stoop.

It is late morning. I am in the city to visit with Grandmother, and hopefully Great Auntie Rose. Momma dropped me off. She needs to take care of things that I'm too young to know about, or not wise enough to keep secret. I am just seven and whatever Momma needs to do, truthfully, I would slow her down. I ring the bell and wait.

"Hello Sherry!" Mrs. Putz yells from across the street.

I smile and wave.

"Visiting your Nana?"

I nod my head, yes. I jump back, as if on cue the door snaps open and Grandmother peeks out, keenly aware of surroundings. She checks the street, nods to Mrs. Putz and ushers me inside. She quickly locks the door.

I trail her lurching motion, up the mahogany staircase. The old curved railing shudders, as she pulls her weight upward. The dark hallway smells of old people and old meals of cabbage and tomatoes.

Up in the kitchen I wait at the table, listening to the ticking kitchen clock and whistling kettle. She pours us a cuppa, and drops slices of buttered bread on the dessert plates between us. I glance up, waiting. Grandmother, only five-foot tall, is very wide and slow. I quickly drop my eyes when she turns towards me.

I watch her broad "immigrant" hands, resting on her lap. In this country fifty years, proudly she will always claim to be an immigrant. Accent, culture, beliefs never gone; never changed; Displayed like a badge of challenge to all comers.

Emily Thompson

Her hands gnarled and thickened from use and arthritis, are always fluttering about, performing some task. Momma says pain keeps Grandmother's hands always in motion.

Her fingers twitch as the reach up to snatch her cup from her saucer, and hold it aloft. Her other hand fiddles with the table, the cup, the doily, the plates.

With my two hands, I can barely manage my half-filled teacup. Carefully, I ape her actions, but set down my cup to nibble my buttered slice of brown bread. I like the brown bread from the bakery down the street.

Bread finished, eyes down, I sit quietly until her attention will center on me. You see, in Grandmother's house you do not speak "out of turn."

She will interrogate me at her leisure, as she interrogates every visitor. The few, the ones lucky enough to gain access to her second floor kitchen, overlooking her back yard filled with chickens and tomato plants, will be treated to the same inquiry. She questions all her visitors, kept outdoors, about neighbors, or strangers they meet. She always wants the tales about the strangers first, before she hears their own stories, if she is so inclined.

I know the drill, and the consequences. Answer all her questions or suffer her shuns. There will be no tea. No buttered bread. No visits to Great Aunt Rose always dressed in white, who lives "down below" on the first floor. No choreographed racing down the block to greet Grandpa when he arrives home. No talking, not even to myself. And no escapes.

Nervous, alone upstairs in her kitchen, waiting Momma's return, I do not feel lucky at all.

I exhale a sigh, waiting and wishing. I long to explore. Not far, not the whole city, not even downtown to Port Arthur or Quackenbush's Department Store. I just want to explore this one block. The other children living on this street are from exotic lands with strange names and different tongues. But there are no journeys outside of this house, except by matriarchal decree.

Grandmother sneezes and my attention snaps back. She wipes her nose on her sleeve-covered arm, starting at her elbow down to her wrist. The whole time never dropping a morsel of bread or spilling any tea.

Her sneeze will not wait for her to retrieve one of Grandfather's cotton handkerchief she always keeps nestled under her dress; tucked under her bra strap. That plaid tissue is only for more serious sneezes and wipes.

I almost look at her face, but remember: never look her in the eye. If I do, she always signs the cross and complains to Momma. Momma says it's because I remind her of someone. We don't know who. Besides Grandmother means nothing by it, Momma says.

I look away at the sound of chewing, then cautiously glance at her hungry mouth. Crumbs sometimes drop from her mouth to her lap, as she greedily chews her chunk of bread. She will manage the crumbs later.

I sit quietly at the kitchen table, still studying her hands. Her fingers are flat and stubby, permanently discolored, tinted red brown, from work. The pads on her fingers are calloused and smooth; no fingerprints to discern. Her hands sometimes jerk, with an involuntary motion. But she manages just fine swatting at her misbehaving dogs, errant grandchildren, or feeding herself.

For years, she worked in a ribbon factory, long since shuttered. She does not miss the work that shaped and challenged her fingers. What she misses, is the gossip of her coworkers and the regiment that promoted her, and eventually displaced her.

The process for manufacturing ribbon was labor-intensive before automation. Workers dyed, treated and wound thread for making the ribbons. Some days she came home with her fingers blue or yellow. But mostly red, since red is the most preferred color for all holidays.

After the ribbon thread is dyed, it is rolled on large bobbins and hoisted to the ceiling, to be used in the many looms throughout the building, weaving the strips of ribbon.

The factory was large. Wooden floors warped and stained by the heavy machinery that clanked and groaned. Machinery that was tended to and caressed by human fingers. Fingers that dyed the thread and kept it flat, machine fed wound on wooden spools. Always ready to be placed and woven. The workers never sat; always walking, preventing problems, prepping looms, keeping the product moving and earning their keep. Inside the factory, there wasn't any talking. Nobody could hear each other over the noise of the machines. Breaks outside and all stories shared, were treasured. Now she has no access to the stories or the story tellers.

Workers, mostly women, had continued as more modern machines were introduced to replace them. Men went on to the better jobs elsewhere.

Automated machines introduced new efficiency and more sophisticated ribbon styles. Human fingers became too costly to reteach or employ. Workers were obsolesced.

These new machines multiplied and grew larger, filling the buildings. Workers and their space diminished, until they were displaced. Then it became cheaper to make things far away, or in strange lands. Shift workers and factories became old, outmoded and forgotten in this town.

Without that outside job, prying about the outside world she never really knew, except through beer halls and speakeasys, became her work. Her spider-like mission to control all existence, through her network of spies and their gleaned information. She was locked out of a world gone modern and a family only too happy to escape states away.

Today, I believe she looks for a connection, to gain some control that was lost. Then, unnerved by her, and her belief, I resemble someone unknown. I strive for inconspicuous. I obey like a good girl.

I watch her hands. Her hands will always be stained and compressed into twisted forms. Her fingers and hands will never return to their original condition. Never soft or straight as when she was young and newly arrived. The youngest of thirteen, father long gone and mother dead, "two weeks afore crossing." Her story was rarely to be spoken of or shared, or remembered by anyone, even before she was gone.

∽

At 65, I sit at my own kitchen table. I look at my own hands. Never delicate or pretty, but always broad, stumpy and strong. My own hands have grown thick and numb; hampered by carpel tunnel, and often stilled. Lately, I find I have been remembering my childhood and my encounters with Grandmother. Often I am lost in those childhood times remembered.

I snort, and again I am staring at her hands, lost in thoughts. Not mine, but thoughts she sometimes spoke; I sometimes heard. Thoughts she sometimes remembered and carelessly shared. Thoughts I now remember.

༄

Her chewing stops. I look up and watch as she carefully pours some tea from her cup into her saucer to drink. Cooled by the shallow piece of china, she holds the saucer to her lips and sips, dainty, pinkies aloft. She turns to me and almost smiles, then remembers I look like someone remembered— never named. She lays aside her empty saucer of tea and milk.

Her fingers, crackling, flutter up adjusting her glasses. She faces me straight on. Staring at my forehead, never looking at me in my eyes.

I am given notice. I am challenged to be ready, for the visit begins now.

✝

A Cat's Tale
Rachel Thompson

It's clear to me now, at the end of my nine lives. As I fade, I understand. Had I known, in the beginning, I would have failed more. I'd have been less of a cat.

When I first met Edward, I was confused. I was a spirit, uncertain of my own nature, trapped inside a young black cat. I was but a kitten, compelled by feline ways.

Many years passed inside that first cat, and the eight cats after that, before I had control enough over my cattishness to know myself. It was better that way, not knowing. I didn't understand that only an innocent could receive Edward's heart, or influence it.

Edward was my reason for being. I know that now.

From the start, I projected feelings into him. For what purpose, I did not know then. We were linked spirits and neither of us knew it. On his deathbed, he still didn't know.

It was 1962 when his mother found me lurking about by the front step. It was then I first realized I was sentient, and I panicked in the knowing—knowing I was a cat but not a cat.

I cried out, "Save me, madam! Remove this cattishness from me." But all that came out was, "meyoll, meyoll."

She bent down and picked me up with mirth. She was a stout woman, young and strong. From her arms I surveyed the world. Her home was a little post-war shit-box, as they called it. That is to say, a long, low ranch house. It was very small indeed.

I looked out from her arms and saw a dirt road carved out of a farmer's field. There were two other houses down the hill that men were building on

103

this street, which was now a ruined cow pasture.

Cows mooed from the field across that fresh gravel road and I hissed all my confusion at them. That field was never subsequently developed. Such was my power, which I didn't yet understand. When I died the second time, Edward's dad buried me there among the cow bones.

"Now, now, what shall I call you?" Edward's mom said, holding me up by my cattish armpits. I dangled there not knowing my own name. "Lucky thing them cows or cement trucks didn't squish you like a slug. Lots of slugs around here. Mice, too. You'll come in handy, lucky for me and lucky for you. That's it! I'll call you Lucky."

Then, she drew me closer with tenderness, cradled me like a new babe, and scratched me behind my ears. A motor of contentment released within me, it felt nice. It felt right to be cattish—for the moment. Other cattish things came to me then. I felt a pang of hunger in my stomach. I tried to tell her, but all that came out was "meyoll."

"Oh, you're hungry I see. Come inside and have a bite. Meet my son and daughter. No school for them yet."

In a panic, I struggled to be put down, but my cattish stomach would not let me run from the idea of food. What could I do? I was a spirit in a flesh body and that body needed sustenance. This much I knew, though I did not know *how* I knew it.

I was whisked into the ranch house. The aluminum screen door snapped behind us as she carried me in. The bang of the door should have frightened me, but I saw a baby playing on the floor, a little boy in a cloth diaper and a little dirty t-shirt. My heart leapt and my body followed. All at once, I knew he was why I had come, but . . . *how* did I know that? I went to him and rubbed my cattish head on his face with joy. He giggled and said, "Kitty, Kitty!"

"Ha! I'm the lucky one," Mother said. "You're just what I need to keep my two-year-old entertained. Lucky meet Edward."

"Meyoll," I said.

She proceeded into the kitchen, which was only a step away from the living room, and opened a can of tuna fish. The smell of it drove me into the kitchen. How disturbing! I had so little control over my own body!

Cattishness was firmly in control, so I gobbled it up before I knew it. When I came to my right mind again, I realized this family was poor. This shabby little house, although new, was cheap, the clothes they wore were rags, and the beat-to-hell furniture was probably picked from the local dump. That can of tuna was a sacrifice. Would her husband be cross when he got in from work?

I decided right then and there I would fend for myself and not cost them any more than necessary. I decided to become a mouser that day—as soon as I was less of a kitten. I dedicated myself to be the little boy's best pal as further repayment.

I had found an awareness of my place in life, although I did not understand exactly what my role was. The cattishness in me ruled my body, usurped my mind, but one thing was clear: I was for that boy Edward and he was for me. Somehow, behind it all, I knew he was my charge. Call it instinct, not cattish instinct, mind you, but an inner knowing.

Over the years of his youth, I taught him humanity such as kindness to animals and others, to love in small ways. I would comfort him when he was spanked, or sick, or had failed his test. I curled at his feet when he drew pictures or read books or watched TV. When he became complacent, I scratched him until he went outside to play. Outside, I'd follow him cattishly and warn him when the mean boy came around.

Edward was deathly afraid of that bully.

Once, when Edward was eleven, I spied the mean boy, Gene, hitting him under the big oak across the street. I quickly climbed the tree and fell upon Gene with raking claws. The bully eventually grabbed me and dashed me to the ground. Edward, inspired, attacked him with doggish courage and Gene withdrew.

From that day onward, Gene would pitch rocks at me and later, shoot at me with his bow and arrows but by that time I had grown so clever, he could never get close enough to cause me harm.

Edward grew into a confident teenager. And that was good, for I became so cattish I was no longer of any help to him. We had the same problem. Edward was distracted with females, as was I. I was the biggest tomcat within half a mile, and as such, always fending off challengers. My ears were nicked, I had scars across my face, and I had ripped out a nail in a fight with a bobcat! Cats and dogs gave way wherever I roamed after that, but, in my pride, I forgot to look after Edward.

Perhaps that is why I died that first time.

I was in the house that day, licking my paws and dressing my most recent wound—a gouge behind my ear where a hound dog had bitten me not long before. Edward came to me. He was seventeen and in need of comfort.

"Lucky," he said, "This girl broke my heart!" He shoved a photograph toward me where I lay. "I don't know if I should shit or spit!"

I was in no mood. The battle was still upon me and my cattishness would not let me think straight. He reached for me, soothingly, and I lashed out. I slashed his hand with a claw.

"God dang cat!" He leapt back. "What's your problem?" He swatted at me the way Mom did when I jumped on the kitchen table.

I stood and hissed, raised the hair on my back. War was upon me again. I did not know what I was doing.

"Great, when I need you, you turn on me. Just like Kathy! Screw you!"

Edward came at me. I tried to run for the cat door but he kicked me viciously on my way out. The blow knocked me through the little flap and over the stoop's edge. I bounced off all three concrete steps on my way to the lawn.

I was badly hurt. At fifteen years old, a cat is practically ancient. My reflexes had failed me or I would have not been so bad off. Such was the blow that it knocked the cattishness right out of me. I lay there panting and thinking—and dying.

Then I remembered why I had come. I had come for Edward and I had failed him in his need. I began to cry in my cattish way. I cried for Edward's pain, I cried for Mom and Dad left to raise two children without a cat. I cried for all of them until a realization bathed me in light. I could not die here! Edward would never forgive himself! But my hip was broken! My guts were bleeding inside of me.

"Edward!" Mom called. "Go see what that fool cat is whining about."

"I'm busy, Mom!"

"I'll give you busy! He's your cat."

"All right, soon as I hang up the phone."

Funny how uncat-like I was in dying. But, one last time, I summoned my cattishness. There was a vent hole through the foundation wall near the stoop. I had long ago pushed the grate out. With my front paws I dragged myself to the hole and crawled through.

"Mom, he's gone, ran off someplace. I'm going over Kathy's."

I heard his footsteps. His car's engine started. The gravel of the driveway crackled, then the chirp of tires on pavement. He was gone. This would not do. They would smell me rotting, so I crawled in the mud until I was well away from the vent hole, and there I passed.

And so my first life ended and I returned in another cat and another. I was always black and they always named me Lucky—all nine of me. But, my luck has now run out.

Edward, seventy-eight years old, died a week ago. All during his cancer treatments I lay in his lap. I did all I could to absorb his sickness to no avail. I got sick, too. I died full of cancer at the foot of his bed just after they took his body away.

Now, I am a spirit again floating free. The Light calls me but I cannot go. I will not go. What of Edward's grandson? Who will watch over him with Edward and me gone? Edward's son had been killed in war, and Edward, such a good man, fought to prevent wars since. It had been his life's work and passion.

Edward had fought the good fight. Who will teach his grandson kindness in this bitter world?

As I hover over Edward's funeral service, the Light grows stronger, pulling me. I can't resist it much longer. How can I rest in peace knowing Edward the Third is alone? I am a failure in my duty to him. I must stay!

But look, the family is leaving the parlor. The Light pulls me so strongly. I am higher now. I know if I don't let go, I will cease to exist as a spirit.

But wait—there is a white cat on the stoop. It follows the little boy. Grandmother grabs him up. As I fade into blackness I hear her say, "Lucky for us you came along, little Edward's going to need a pal."

I let go and all became light.

✝

Running Buddy
Diane VanDyke

T he Nuss family was going to visit the National Aquarium in Baltimore. Tabbi couldn't wait. She loved the aquarium, but the last time she was there was six years ago when she was only eight years old. Excited about the visit, she studied the exhibits on the website and made a mental list of what she wanted to see. Sea turtles topped her list, followed by dolphins and then the animals in an exhibit called the Amazon River Forest.

The trip was a special treat. Tabbi's family didn't visit many new places, since her older sister, Sandra, had autism, and she would get distressed by unfamiliar environments, loud noises and crowds. She often would have meltdowns that started with whimpering and crying and then would escalate into full wailing with her arms flapping. If her parents couldn't calm her down by refocusing her attention by listening to music with her cell phone and earphones or even hugging Baxter, her bear pillow pet, they would have to leave.

Tabbi was hopeful this visit would be different. First of all, it was organized and hosted by the Pennville Autism Awareness Association (PAAA), a local autism support group for families. Second, PAAA made special arrangements with the Aquarium so families with children with autism could visit the aquarium in the evening, after it was closed to the public. This would mean fewer people, no lines and less noise. *At least no one would be staring if Sandra starts to cry,* Tabbi thought, since all the participating families would be familiar with autism.

A day before the visit, Tabbi's mom told Sandra about the trip and showed her the fish and other sea life on the Aquarium's website. She explained to Sandra how pretty and peaceful the aquarium would be with the soft lights. Sandra seemed interested and smiled at the pictures, but sometimes it was difficult to know what she understood.

Finally, Saturday evening arrived. They ate at home, rather than risk Sandra becoming agitated from the noise and other sensory stimulation in a restaurant environment. Mom made Sandra's favorite meal—homemade macaroni and cheese. After an uneventful meal, they left for the one-hour drive to the aquarium.

As they got closer, Dad explained to Sandra they would soon be at the aquarium with the pretty fish, trying to ease any fears. After they parked and went inside, they were greeted by Amanda Polin, president of PAAA, who also had a son on the autism spectrum. Only a few other families had arrived by that time. *Ok,* thought Tabbi, *so far, so good.*

Sandra was happy, or at least she wasn't crying. Slowly, however, her expression changed as she looked around. She looked scared.

Seeing her face, the Nuss family quickly headed to the sea turtle exhibit, hoping Sandra would be interested in seeing the turtle to calm any rising anxiety. Tabbi instantly spotted an immense sea turtle, gracefully swimming through the tank, as if it were almost flying in the water. But as she watched it effortlessly glide through the water, she heard her sister start to whimper. *No, not yet,* thought Tabbi, not another family trip to be cut short because of her sister's autism.

Trying to interest Sandra in the fish and other aquatic life to calm her and avoid a meltdown, the Nuss family moved to the next room with an exhibit with several large fish and blue lights. They sat down on the bench to watch the fish and listen to the soft music in the room, hoping it would be enough to relax her. But, Sandra didn't care. Her whimpers turned into crying, which intensified and her face turned red.

"I'll take her through this exhibit," Dad said. "And, then we'll go to the car if she doesn't get better. You and Mom keep going and find the dolphins, okay, Tabbi?"

They rushed off. Sandra's crying started to reach the pitch of no return —it sounded uncontrollable. Tabbi's stomach knotted, and they knew they had about 10 minutes to find and see the dolphins. She checked the map on her Aquarium phone app and guided Mom along until they reached the tanks. The dolphins immediately came up to the glass. Tabbi took photos with her phone. "Mom, let's get a selfie together," said Tabbi standing next to the tank. She saw her mother's head was down and she was texting on her own phone.

"We have to go, Tabbi. Dad's waiting in the car," said Mom.

She put her phone away and reluctantly followed Mom to the lobby. She blinked hard and kept her head down, so Mom would not see her tears. She couldn't help but feel disappointed since their visit was less than a half-hour long, and she barely saw anything.

The ride home wasn't fun either, as Sandra continued to cry, even as she hugged, the not-so-fluffy-anymore Baxter. Tabbi didn't say anything, although she was upset. *Would she ever get to see the Aquarium and other places with her family?*

Eventually, Sandra's sobs stopped, as she retreated to her own world. Tabbi was too caught up in her own thoughts to notice, though, as she thought about the sea creatures and other exhibits she didn't get to see.

∽

When they arrived home, Mom and Dad took Sandra inside to go to bed. Tabbi, however, saw a brown package on the porch that no one else noticed earlier that day. She walked over and picked up the package. It was from her running buddy, Ms. Katrina Moyer, who lived in Pennsylvania.

Ms. Moyer and Tabbi, as well as Tabbi's family, participated in an organization called, "Running Buddies," which connects runners with children with disabilities and their siblings. Sandra had her own buddy, who posted messages on the closed group Facebook page and sent her race medals and little gifts. Ms. Moyer became Tabbi's running buddy several months ago and also sent her race medals and messages.

Seeing the package lifted her spirits, especially after such a crummy evening, Tabbi didn't stop to tell her parents. She ripped off the tape and opened the box. Inside, was a medal from Ms. Moyer's recent half-marathon, the Rock 'n' Roll Half-Marathon in Philadelphia. The medal was in the shape of the Liberty Bell and featured a mass of runners on Benjamin Franklin Parkway. The quarter-inch medal was heavy and had a blue ribbon on it with the words, "Half-Marathon." Tabbi put it on and tried to image what it was like running a half-marathon and crossing the finish line.

Under the medal in the box was a card with her name on it and a pack of her favorite candy. She opened the card and read the message. Ms. Moyer described how difficult it was to keep running during the last miles when she was exhausted and sore and how Tabbi was her inspiration to finish. "During the last mile, I was very tired and not sure I could keep going. However, I thought about you, Tabbi, and how you are such a strong, patient sister. You inspired me to cross the finish line. So, I'm giving you this medal because you deserve it," she wrote.

Tabbi looked at the medal and thought about the failed family trip to the aquarium—one of many interrupted, unfinished family activities. She loved her sister and wanted her to be happy. *Visiting an aquarium isn't more important than Sandra,* she thought. *But we'll just keep going, and we'll cross the finish line too.* Tabbi went inside to show the medal to Mom and Dad and to add it to her collection. More than the medal, though, she loved having a friend who was running for her.

✝

Connecting the Dots
Carol L. Wright

S hut up in a dusty attic was about the last place I wanted to be on the first really sunny Saturday of the spring. But how could I say no?

"Dory, dear," my mom had said when she called. "I need your help."

I knew when she added "dear" to my name she was making an offer I couldn't refuse.

"I'll be over around ten, Doe," I said, using the nickname everyone called her, including us kids.

"And bring some trash bags," she added just as I hung up the phone.

I was the only one of my mom's six kids who had not completely left the nest, so to speak. The others had gone off to various colleges, married people from far away, and established careers in other states. But my parents divorced in my last year of high school, so I lived at home and went to the local community college.

Oh, don't get me wrong; I don't still live at home. I moved last year, when I was twenty-five, to share a townhouse with two of my friends from high school. I was still the only family who lived in town—and the only one that she called when she needed help with anything.

When I arrived that morning, Doe was at least a little apologetic. "Thank you, sweetheart. I know it's not what you'd like to be doing. But I have to get the house ready to . . ." She couldn't finish the sentence. Doe had grown up in that house. It belonged to her grandparents, for heaven's sake. She loved every square inch—creaky floors, noisy pipes, and drafty windows included. But now she had to sell because, in a fit of matrimonial optimism, she put my dad's name on the deed. Now he wanted "his share" of the money out of it. No way my mom could buy him out, so she had to sell her family legacy and the only place she—or I—had ever really called home.

"It's just that," she continued, steadying her voice, "I feel like losing this house is like losing my mother and grandmother all over again."

It made me sick to think about it. Each of us kids had taken a crack at Dad, trying to get him to change his mind. "Financial reverses" was his only answer. He needed the money.

So today, I was going to go up into the attic to try to cull the must-keeps from the why-did-we-save-*theses*. I figured that there would be a lot more of the latter.

Truth be told, I thought it might be fun. You know—find an old item tucked away by great-grandma that would bring tens of thousands on *Antiques Roadshow*? I mean, my family was never rich, but geez—they had to have *something* worth keeping to have filled up an entire attic, right? If I could find it, Doe could stay.

So, armed with a cold bottle of water and a fresh box of trash bags, I picked my way up the cluttered staircase. Everything from hubcaps to metal milk jugs blocked the path, daring me to make my way to the top. When I got there, I was pleased that I could stand upright—at least down the center of the space.

Any thoughts I had of an authentic Tiffany lamp or Chippendale bureau or long-lost Vermeer died when I saw the stacks of dusty trunks and sagging boxes stacked willy-nilly under the sloping rafters. They nearly obliterated the meager light that came through the smudged-up windows at the gable ends. Fortunately, despite a collection of dented oil lamps, somewhere along the line someone ran electricity up here, so I had a bare bulb to see by—probably one of Edison's first.

A-a-a-a-CHOO! I never was too good with dust and this place was musty enough to give the Statue of Liberty asthma.

I unscrewed the cap of the water bottle and took a swig. *Okay*, I told myself. *It might be no picnic for you, but it's better than having Doe do it.* It made me feel a bit noble, and helped me get down to it.

By noon, I had gone through enough boxes to begin sorting them by type: cardboard boxes full of disintegrating newspapers (most of which had become mouse condos, sad to say); books and magazines from who knows how long ago that were growing a mold of some sort; and broken stuff. And by broken stuff, I mean all kinds: chairs with loose legs, a rocking horse with broken springs (and peeling paint that *had* to have lead in it), TVs in need of tubes they stopped making during the Nixon Administration; tools with broken handles; and a host of discarded toasters, lamps, blenders, shoe-shine machines, electric frying pans, and some things that I'm not really sure *what* they were. Beyond those was the most special category of all: stray pieces of stuff. I swear, my ancestors never threw anything out. If there was any chance that a screw, bolt, fitting, pipe, board, or twist-tie could be used again, it was preserved. It was then I realized this wasn't my mother's attic; it was junk heaven.

When Doe called up to see if I wanted lunch, I was glad to get back downstairs where I could inhale air I couldn't see. I'd check with her to see if we could get a dumpster delivered—and position it right below the attic window.

"Oh, Dory, you have cobwebs in your hair," she said, picking at the schmutz that had made me prematurely gray.

"That's the least of it," I said, rolling my eyes for effect. Then I saw her expression. It wasn't just sadness I saw there; it was grief. This was harder on her than she wanted to let on—even to me.

As I munched my turkey sandwich with mayo and cream cheese—don't knock it until you try it—I thought about what clearing out the attic meant to her. To me it was junk; to Doe it was her family—her whole life. I *had* to find something of value that she could sell and buy Dad's share of the house.

I started in after lunch with renewed enthusiasm—and my iPad. Anything that looked like it might have intrinsic value got Googled. I didn't want to be one of those fools who let a priceless *whatever* get sold at a yard sale for two dollars. But the more I dug through piles and boxes, the less optimistic I became. Even in mint condition, the antiques I found were pretty common and not worth much. And the stuff in this attic was seldom in mint condition. But I was determined to keep looking.

By Sunday night, I had looked into every box, moved every pile, and dug through every stack of odds and ends. Nothing. No treasure that would enable Doe to keep the house. There was just one trunk left to open. From the size of it, I knew it wouldn't hold anything large. What could possibly fit in there that would be valuable enough to save her home? Coins? Jewelry? My people weren't the kind to have a treasure horde. Could an antique clock or lamp of sufficient value be locked inside? Only one way to find out.

I wiped my dirty hands on my jeans. There was a padlock on the trunk, but no key. I had been finding loose keys for two days. *Where did I put them?*

I found the bin I'd used to hold small items that might be of some use and dug through. I found old skeleton keys, car keys, house keys, and luggage keys. There were only five keys, though, that might fit the padlock on the trunk. I tried the first. No—of course it wasn't the one. In such situations, you always need to try all five before you find the correct one, right? That is, if you actually have the correct one at all. So, I tried the second. It jiggled just a little in the lock. My heart skipped a beat.

"Where is that WD-40?" I asked aloud, looking around. I found the can and shook it up, hoping the propellant would still work. I popped the cap and sprayed the snot out of that lock. I inserted the key again. It wiggled a little more than before. I knelt next to the trunk, leaned against the lid, and bore down with all the force my tired fingers could manage.

It opened. *It opened!*

I removed the lock from the hasp, and undid the latches. I was almost afraid to lift the lid. This was my last chance to be a heroine.

I yanked it open.

Paper. That stupid trunk was filled with stacks of notebooks and loose paper. I knew that unless one of them was a copy of the Magna Carta, Doe was screwed.

I took out one of the broken chairs. With a couple of screws from the loose junk box, I was able to make it stable enough for my purposes. Then I pulled out an old floor lamp with frayed wiring. I was sure I had seen . . . Sure enough, there was lamp cord in the "perhaps-salvageable" box. I was able to make a quick job of rewiring and plugging the lamp into the lone outlet under the window. I turned the switch and—no—of course the old light bulb had blown. But there was a box of incandescent bulbs up there, too. In a few moments—light! A lot of it. It must have been a hundred-watt bulb. So I dug around until I found an old maroon, chenille lampshade, complete with frayed ball fringe along the bottom. Hideous, but utilitarian.

I pulled the lamp over to the chair, and picked up the first few sheets. There was cursive writing all over it—a bit flowery—in what now looked like light brown ink. *Must be old.*

❧

"What is it?" Doe asked.

My Cheshire cat grin and hands held behind my back must have alerted her to my excitement at my discovery. "Sit down," I said, keeping my treasure behind me to prevent her getting a look at what I was concealing.

She sat on the chintz sofa, and I moved to sit next to her, but she put up an arm. "No you don't, sister. Not in those dirty pants. Get a towel before you sit on my sofa."

I obeyed, and, when I was finally next to her, said, "Now close your eyes and hold out your hands." She looked at me sideways, but did as I asked.

"What did you find?" she asked. "You're being very mysterious."

"These," I said, placing a stack of small books into her hands.

She opened her eyes and held the stack up close to her face. I knew the musty smell of those old books was a little off-putting, but it wasn't the smell that made me bring them down to her. "What are these?" I think she hoped I found first editions of Shakespeare's folios, but, of course, my people wouldn't have those, either.

"They're diaries," I said, trying to keep the triumph out of my voice.

"Diaries? Whose?" Doe put the stack in her lap and picked up the top volume, opening it to the fly leaf. She gasped. "Dorothea. Why she's, she's my great-great-grandmother!"

"Yes! And some from her daughter, and even a few from her granddaughter."

"I never knew they were there. I didn't think we had any papers of Dorothea's. Just the old stories handed down."

"I know. I've heard them all my life. How she came to the United States after the Civil War with nothing but the goods she could carry and a two-year-old daughter in hand."

"That daughter was my great-grandmother, Thea," Doe said nodding. "Dorothea started a dressmaking business, and built it up to be one of the most successful in the city." She had a far-off look in her eye. "But none of her work survived except that pillow I've saved for you."

"There are some of Dorothea's patterns in there, too."

Her eyes grew wide. "I almost thought the whole story was just a family legend."

"And in each generation since, a daughter has been named 'Dorothea' in her honor," I said. "Me, you, Grandma Dot, Great-grandma Dottie, and Thea. It's a long chain," I said, feeling like I was part of something big and important.

She put her hand against my cheek. "I almost broke that chain. I didn't give the name to either of your sisters, but somehow, when you were born, it just seemed like I'd been saving it for you all along."

"Aw," I said, giving her a hug. We both blinked back tears for a moment. Then I remembered I had something else to show her. "That's not all," I said, flourishing a photo in a metal frame from behind my back, magician-style. "We have her picture." I held up the image of a young woman, dressed in all black—Victorian widow's weeds—with a young girl at her side. On the bottom, their names were written in what I now knew to be Dorothea's handwriting, and the date: 1872.

Now the tears really flowed. "I never saw a photo of her," Doe said.

"Even without their names, I'd know that the little girl must be Thea. I only knew her as a *very* old woman, but I can see the determined expression in her eyes."

I scrutinized the child's face, trying to make it look like Doe or me or Grandma Dot. "I don't see a resemblance," I said.

Doe pursed her lips. "Perhaps not," she said, but then turned to me with an arched brow. "But surely you can see something else?"

I studied the photo in a way I hadn't when I found it in the attic. It was a typical late-1800s photo—stiff bodies, unsmiling faces. The clothes were typical of the age. But then I studied Dorothea's face. "She looks kind of familiar," I said.

"Oh, Dory," Doe said. "She's you!"

～◦

I never found a treasure that saved Doe's house. She sold it and with her share, paid cash for a condo. But what I did find enabled Doe to take our family with her. It was worth much more than an old house with creaky floorboards, noisy pipes, and drafty windows. I found a connection to our ancestors—and an even stronger connection to my mom.

✝

Essays

Imagine, *Revisited*
Beverly Botelho

When John Lennon released the song "Imagine" in 1971, he called for a world without countries, religions, and conspicuous consumption. He claimed that such a world is within our grasp. Yet, over four decades later, his vision still just that: imaginary.

We human beings are the only species to have developed a sophisticated combination of visual and aural symbols for communication. Through the arts we have the potential to transcend virtually every boundary and border that exists. I believe we should use the arts to foster peace, cooperation and inclusion.

In his "Book of Joy," Archbishop Desmond Tutu recounts his historic visit with His Holiness, the Dalai Lama. Two Nobel Peace Prize Laureates meet for the first time. It demonstrated to me that people from different races, classes, cultures, countries and religions can come together to learn from each other and to gain a deeper respect for another's perspective.

Archbishop Desmond Tutu, retired religious leader and prominent social and human rights activist observed about people, "You are made for perfection, but you are not yet perfect. You are a masterpiece in the making." The Archbishop looks at us as a vision of possible perfection.

Tenzin Gyatso, the 14th Dalai Lama is the exiled leader of the Tibetan people and Tibetan Buddhism. His Holiness, a social rights activist in his own right, envisions peace from a different perspective. He believes that everyone wants happiness, nothing more. Like other Buddhists, he believes suffering is inevitable, but he sees suffering not as something to bemoan or endure, but as something to rejoice in. "The suffering is what makes you appreciate joy," he said.

The Write Connections

During their time together, these remarkable men demonstrated the cooperation and respect that humans are capable of. They reverently shared traditions usually exclusive to members of their own respective religions. At the same time, they reflected on their common experiences. They laugh heartily, cry, and experience anger. They are, after all, human.

I see their meeting as a starting point. I, too, can welcome people different from me. There's no need to feel threatened by differences. Their contributions—scientific, cultural, political, religious and/or commercial enrich the world. Every day, I have the opportunity to reap an overflowing cornucopia of unfamiliar viewpoints and experiences first hand. I can gain it from across the garden gate or in the form of an account written by the survivor of terrorism, ostracism or exclusion. I am the recipient of another's point of view. As these two venerable leaders demonstrated, we are enriched, personally, by respecting another's point of view.

Imagine a world as one. I can. I can see a world where people live with and for the textured world of the other. I see the world as a virtual closet of different cloaks, coats and robes of many colors, designs and styles. And it's always roomy enough to include one more.

✝

Miracles
Mike Boushell

According to Merriam-Webster's, a miracle is an extraordinary event manifesting divine intervention in human affairs. The event is often believed to be caused by the power of God. It surpasses all known human or natural powers. Thus, it is ascribed to a supernatural intervention because it is inexplicable according to existing natural or scientific laws.

That definition makes sense to those that believe in the powers of God, but just how and why do miracles occur? Moreover, are we still living in the age of miracles, as when Jesus Christ walked the earth and was responsible for incredible healings, even raising the dead to life? Since I died at the age of five, I can affirm that indeed this continues to be the age of miracles.

It was 1950. My uncle had just finished working his construction job when he agreed to take me swimming with him at Stokes Mill, a popular swimming hole in Brodhead's Creek. Upon arrival, my uncle cautioned me to wait for him until he finished visiting with a few friends on the opposite bank. I nodded my agreement, but soon grew bored and decided to soothe my burning feet in the nearby shallows while he chatted with his pals. I never thought I was disobeying him, I just needed to cool my feet. Slowly, I edged my way into the refreshing water.

The next thing I remember, I was looking down from above at what appeared to be a crowd of people gathered around a small boy who looked a lot like me. My uncle was crying. He pleaded with the boy to breathe and open his eyes, but the boy was lying very still. I don't think the boy was able to hear him.

As I watched, I remember feeling very calm—completely unafraid—a bright light engulfing me. At no time did I feel any pain or trepidation. Instead, I just closed my eyes and slept—a lot.

When I finally woke, I was lying in a hospital bed, a plastic tent enclosing me. My mother stood nearby peering down at me, a smile on her face, tears streaming down her cheeks. My father stood beside her, smiling and holding an armful of comic books. He later explained he had been reading them to me for several hours each day. I hadn't heard any of it.

My mother said I was inside an oxygen tent and air was being blown inside to make my breathing easier. The doctor had told them I had double pneumonia and they should hope for the best, but expect the worst. Back then, double pneumonia was usually "a death sentence." My mother and father refused to believe the worst would happen. Instead, they prayed—for nearly two weeks.

What happened to me may or may not have been a miracle, but sixty-five years later, I choose to believe it was. My five children and seven grandchildren believe in miracles too.

✝

Six Degrees of Samuel Clemens
John Evans

In the early '90s, while putting some finishing touches on a book about *Tom Sawyer*, I went to Hannibal, Missouri, to photograph local scenes and do some final research. One item on my agenda was to look into the character of Injun Joe, the villainous half-breed killer of the novel. Much of *The Adventures of Tom Sawyer* is autobiographical and many of the characters were drawn from life. Injun Joe, it is believed, was modeled after a citizen of Hannibal—an Osage Indian who, as a child, survived being scalped by Pawnees. A cowboy rescued him and raised him as a son, then set him off on his own.

Named for his benefactor, Joe Douglas settled in Hannibal, Missouri, where he lived until his death in 1923. With a red bandana worn to cover his scars, Injun Joe became an easily recognized local character—a Native American living in a small Midwestern community.

During my research, I came upon a local historian, J. Hurley Hagood, a life-long resident of Hannibal who gave me more background on Injun Joe and directed me to his grave in the local cemetery. As our conversation wound down, Mr. Hagood told me that when he was a young boy, Hannibal held a celebration of Mark Twain. Being a Boy Scout, he was assigned to be the personal attendant to Laura Hawkins Frasier, Twain's boyhood sweetheart and the model for Becky Thatcher.

Long after my book was published, and thoughts of Injun Joe and J. Hurley Hagood were shelved for more pressing business, I happened upon "Six Degrees of Kevin Bacon" on a TV show. Using the theory that everyone in the world is connected within six relationships, two trivia buffs were challenged to link Kevin Bacon to other actors in the film industry. As

I watched, it suddenly occurred to me that I was connected to Samuel Clemens! I knew J. Hurley Hagood, who knew Laura Hawkins Frazier, who was Samuel Clemens's childhood sweetheart—with just two degrees of separation. My mind raced with Twain's connections: Thomas Edison, Nikola Tesla, Ulysses S. Grant, Harriet Beecher Stowe, Helen Keller, Theodore Roosevelt, and countless other writers and dignitaries. I was also linked to them and their acquaintances with plenty of degrees to spare.

I came to view myself as mankind's portal to the past, and I sometimes gently steered conversations to a place where I could share my good fortune. And, with my spare degrees, I was able to bestow upon my friends a position of nearly equal importance.

"I'm connected to Mark Twain," I told a colleague during one of those conversations, and I explained my connection.

"Me, too," she countered. "I have a picture of my grandmother as a child sitting on Twain's lap."

"Oh . . ."

I could feel my important place in the universe crumbling.

I guess we *are* all connected—more than anyone would ever think.

✝

Mere Stones
Jennifer Lader

While our storytelling can reshape the past and present, occasionally something happens to set events in stone, connecting them to future generations forever.

On a recent visit to Roosevelt Island—a lesser-known part of New York City—I noticed stones lay nearly everywhere. They covered the shores. Some crumbled in heaps amidst moldering ruins, others more orderly, graced the island's tip, bright white marble monoliths.

This island, narrow and only two miles in length, lies in the East River that courses alongside New York City. Originally home to the Lenni Lenape tribe, the island became a pig farm and then the quarantine zone for the city's sick residents. The masonry of the vine-choked walls at the abandoned Smallpox Hospital adheres, barely, as a testament to the days when the wealthy could be drawn to a sanatorium, if it was ornate enough. In the 1920s, the place came to be known as "Welfare Island," site of low-income housing. Then that term fell out of favor.

Franklin D. Roosevelt also served as the governor of New York State, so when the time came in 1973 to find a new moniker for the island, the natural choice was "Roosevelt." Less natural, and so all the more incredible, is that a buildout of earth and rock should be created to extend the southern tip of the island, putting it on par with the United Nations complex. The architect, Louis Kahn designed the grounds and monument to be installed on that extension in memory of Roosevelt. The complex rose, inspired in its foundation by what FDR called, in his 1941 State of the Union speech, "four essential freedoms." These are freedom of speech and self-expression, freedom to worship as one chooses, freedom from want, and freedom from fear. Unfortunately, the memorial is listed among Kahn's "unbuilt" works.

Not so any more.

The linden tree-lined Four Freedoms Park, completed in 2012, features optical illusions along paths that lead to an outdoor "room" of stone, sunlight, and serenity. All this, even though the ceiling-less monument lies exposed to the river and to the cityscapes of Manhattan and Queens. I can see a red Pepsi-Cola sign lashed to a row of bleak apartment buildings. There is the certain knowledge that, to the west in Midtown, car horns and sirens call out their warnings. Yet, those sounds are muted.

The very walls of the memorial encouraged tunnel vision. I look to the river, the walls seem to whisper. Though they feel permanent, water will wear down any stone. The haze in the air that day gradually obscured the sights on the opposite banks. It diminished the glare of not only the sun, but also of my busy mind.

My thoughts drifted while my body relaxed onto the summer-warmed white marble couch. I gazed off the Memorial's stern right angles and into the river. There, sea gulls huddled on water-smoothed rocks, as if waiting to see what else will be built of mere stone.

✝

An Unexpected Gift
Donna Searle McLay

When I was in sixth grade, my baby brother Dick was born, the fifth child in our family. As the eldest, I had a unique position: mother's helper. I played with Dick, sang to him, took him for walks, changed his diapers, and read to him. We enjoyed Beatrix Potter's animal tales as well as Howard R. Garis' stories, *Uncle Wiggily Longears* and *Lulu Alice and Jimmie Wibblewobble,* among others. Dick grew into a smart, witty, gentle, talented man, and we try to see each other a couple of times a year even though we're separated by several hundred miles.

Dick entered first grade the year that I went to college. After graduating from Slippery Rock in 1958, I returned to Sharpsville for my first teaching job: fifth grade in South Pymatuning Elementary School, the elementary school in the country. Dick was attending one of the elementary schools in town. All the district's students came together for grades 7-12 and were graduated from Sharpsville High School in 1966.

I was invited to the 50th class reunion of the Class of 1966, and sat at a round table for ten with my brother Dick and our spouses, among others. What a festive evening! There was much talk of how the students had fared in life. I had fond memories of teaching art, music, and p. e., because this was before the days of the specialists in elementary school. We played dodge ball and kickball, and took carpet samples outside to sit on while we sketched trees and other landscapes; we studied all the usual subjects, and added the stories of the constellations in the night sky to our knowledge.

After dinner, while introductions and speeches were going on, I was surprised to see a former student, Cheryl Bennett, rush in and make a beeline for our table. She was supposed to be at a golf tournament!

"I had to come," she said. "I was going to crash the gate if they wouldn't let me in. It's because of you that I became a teacher."

I was both honored and stunned. We hugged. "What did you teach?" I asked.

"Math," she said. "We had such fun in your class, with stories and plays and music and art and all those dodge ball games! I remember you taught me about the stock market. That got me really interested in math. I taught elementary, middle school, and high school math, and retired in 2015." Yes, most of these "kids" were retired.

"Cheryl," I said, "you know that teaching is like dropping pebbles into a pond. The ripples go out and we hardly ever hear back. So thank you for telling me this. You made my day!"

She replied, "You made my life!"

✝

Thoughts at the End of the Day
David A. Miller, II

Sept. 11, 2001 - 9:30 PM

New York City is impossibly silent tonight. I'm still here only because the Port Authority building is locked. No way to get to Pennsylvania.

From my office window, I see at least twelve TV sets across 47th St., all with flickering blueish pictures. They click, click, click through the channels, all showing the same devastating fireballs, grey-coated gasping humans, ambulances and solemn pronouncements.

Our world disintegrated this morning when someone yelled that a plane crashed into the World Trade Tower. I promptly recalled the bomber that crashed into the Empire State Building during WWII. I barely got my 15 seconds of fame.

I shut up in mid-pontification when the first horrendous CNN photo hit the screen, showing the gaping hole in Tower 1. Minutes later, the second plane's fireball was captured and repeated uncounted times. CNN's site was overwhelmed.

New York LIVES on news. Nothing is too much. No coverage is enough, no scoop too large or tiny. Yet the day overwhelmed. Minute by minute, someone would run down the hall with another impossible update. "It can't be." But it was. And it didn't end.

A Senior Partner at our accounting firm, RSSM, had the presence of mind to order in food "in case our people would need it tonight." Much appreciated. Those who could get home (somehow) were allowed to go. To us others, "You're probably safer here than at Port Authority." Our stomachs churned with the impossibility of that grim reality.

The Write Connections

An absolutely perfect morning, with air as soft and warm as an Aruba sunrise, had coalesced into the pervasive smell of cement dust and the sickening knowledge of impending and monstrous death.

Our uptown office has a splendid view straight down Third Avenue. This afternoon, all lanes were full of silent northbound traffic. A pickup truck got a flat tire. A group pushed it to the curb lane then, helped change the tire. Nobody talked. Just did it because it was the right thing to do.

Both sidewalks were eight-wide of humans, walking north as fast as they could without running. Nervous laughter. Many tries on cell phones that didn't work. People walking together would stop, hug, cry, dab their eyes and shuffle along again. Men in expensive business suits, hair and face covered with the deathly pall of white silt, made their way north. Their eyes had died. They just wanted to get away. *Please God.*

We, the lucky ones, came down to the street, compelled to put our own eyes on the rising pall of billowing smoke from the downtown disaster. We tried (unsuccessfully) not to stare at the survivors. Wanted to say something to them, but had no earthly idea of what the words would be. Would have patted them on the shoulder . . . just because, but that certainly would have been . . . so presumptuous. They trudged past us in their grief. We could do nothing to comfort them.

✝

Poems

Essential Pleasures
Beatriz Eugenia Arias

My precious treasures,
they sit upon an antique dresser,
which has its own special past.

Green as the forest, once a tree,
with its scent long gone,
rough to the fingertips,
yet elegant with
its wrought-iron handles
and decorative knobs.

A photograph in an eclectic frame
with all the faces, joyful pleasures,
fondest moments of all those dearest,
and the music box with soothing sounds,
tingly feelings flow, when it's wound,
this, a transformative moment,
which takes me back in time.

And the ornamental book with worn cover,
revealing inside tender care of those words,
on fibrous substance,
of the magnificent Master
that is still with us.

The Write Connections

They, which hold such value,
so many memories, and
so much are they loved.

Those precious treasures,
ah, so they are, they are
my essential pleasures.

Interconnection
Beverly Botelho

I sip a cup of tea, watch TV comedy
While in a world far from mine
A child hugs a distended belly
And chases flies from her eyes.

A kidnapped boy holds a rifle
While cutting off his tears and
Sharp-shooting his fears.

Extended connection yields increasing distraction,
Frustrated compassion thwarts a move to action.
I have only my pen so I write as witness,
Juror and judge.

I vow that before I die I will uncover the mass of bodies
And speak for the dumb.
I will drum 'til the rain falls on the parched plains
and massage the weapons from the terrorist's frozen palms.

If each child were a blank page I would write
Innocence, satiety, peace and alms. This I cannot ensure,
so I write to thaw concern and action
from those frozen with frustrated compunction.

Night Sounds
Mike Boushell

Time was, is, will be,
'til all the shadows pass.
Or, the plastic cross that fastens my hands and feet
at last,
cracks.
Then come the Night Sounds—
quiet, not quite silent sounds.
Signals to sleep sounds,
signs to find release sounds.
Lying there, I listen.
Outside a winter wind pounds an angry fist
upon my window.
Night birds cling to warming cable wires.
Field mice squirm through broken cellar windows.
Tree limbs moan like secret lovers.
And I hear *nothing*.
Inside, there is no sound
save for the crawling of an up-the-wall terrified
spider.
And the beating of its heart
might be mine.

✝

Movement
Ilissa Jae Ducoat

There is someone next to me painting a scene of my own internal workings. Each brush stroke fills in my own picture, a kindred spirit paint by number.

Vibrant, and resonating.

Their words fill the space and I take them in, like inhaling the scent of something baking.

Unique to the moment, yet it stirs my own associations with sweetness or yearning.

My hand on their shoulder, I open my heart and allow them a piece of what they meant to me for the last few moments.

Connection.

More movement.

Someone's hand now touches me. Their words unfold a lotus of similarities and synchronicity, and I see such beauty in something they have tended to for so long, and may not have shared often.

Vulnerable out in the open air, but all of us shall keep it safe.

A room full of words, and energy.

My tribe.

The Write Connections

We fight our fight alone, yet standing beside one another.

We borrow war paint, and perhaps some arrows.

We may not see each other's entire battle, but hands are always outstretched if we get knocked down.

In time, they may notice my wounds, which inspire them to show me theirs.

The act alone is healing.

Movement.

We take our separate journeys, yet can gain so much by walking alongside each other, talking, sharing some strides.

Moving, connecting, resonating.

Allowing.

This is the power of the group.

✝

The Connection
Robert Martin

The spirit within, that sacred place,
Secrets of heaven, written upon the face,
Where beauty and knowledge avail themselves
To who shall seek, ringing in the bells.
I am those words thrown away on purpose.
Gone but not forever, rising to the surface.

Solitude is a lonely peace, looking through windows,
Sheltered in cathedrals where the spirit grows.
Beautiful words flowing from sacred crests,
Up where skies are busy and where heaven rests,
Looking down at empty souls through teary eyes,
To be gathered in a satchel, the words of the wise.

Poets of the sacred order, take heed.
Take to the heavens as you mount your steed.
I'll give you my thoughts as you search the skies.
You'll find the connection where beauty lies.
Heaven and earth bind together on your ride.
Laudations draw near when you look inside.
Your soul is a garden with the jasmine growing,
So sayeth sweet hidden voices in their rising.

The throne of beauty is yours to inherit,
To fill your bones with a resounding merit.
Words come at you from an exotic world
With familiar lines but so gracefully curled.

The Write Connections

They bind your heart with golden strings about
And flood your soul with a triumphant shout.
Hail to the poet! Sweet sounds of sacred talk.
Lift your head high on your spiritual walk,
For thou art a master, a slave, and a lover,
Up where heaven abodes and angels hover.
Into the midst of storied clouds in their swirl
As you shut the door to the familiar world.

You reached the connection where beauty sings,
Riding into dreams on the angels' wings,
Breaking down rhetoric into a lyrical verse,
Where love, passion, and dreams immerse.
Thou sainted poet, you live among the few
who gather at the river in the Almighty's view.

You can declare yourself a poet by God,
Walking forth with thy staff and thy rod
With beauty whispering words in your ear,
As new thoughts and revelations come clear.

There is a burning bush deep down inside
With the lore of the heavens in the flame.
Put down your fears and let your spirit ride.
There's a new you to lift up and acclaim.
A poet, by God, one anointed such as thee.

A Tree Falls
Veronica Mattaboni

If I exist and there is
no one around
to validate me,
did I ever exist
in the first place?

This is a question
only the trees can answer.
So I bury my roots deep final in the underbrush,
turn my branches toward the sun and tell myself:
It's okay to fall.
How else will you learn
to pick yourself back up?

Maybe I don't know how to fix this yet,
but at least I'm asking the right questions.

A Most Silent Lane
David A. Miller, II

In a world of wars and hate-laced words
by our leaders and those who plan their death,
there are few places on our battered earth
to find a bit of peace, save a lane like this.

The wind has calmed. And so, these sturdy trees
are fortunate to keep their white snow decoration
on a grey and chilly December afternoon.
They stand in silence, as they ever have.

Until the car door slams, as children run and shout,
pointing to this tree, no, this other one is prettier,
so, please can we have this one for our home?
Before they even ask, they know what the answer will be.

So home it goes, to be raised and then turned
and decorated with treasures and trinkets
out of memory boxes from so many years ago.
Everyone sings or hums the carols, known so well.

All year, we humans wreck our small blue planet
and blame "the others" for all *their* sins,
while *we* don the bright mantle of true Christmas,
and warble "Hallelujah!" beside our beautiful tree.

146

Growing Older
Dawn M. Sooy

Time, for me, passes quickly.
Days pass swiftly.
Brown hair turns to gray.
"That's life!" they say.

I reminisce about my life.
A mom, a wife.
Children now grown.
Life's new milestone.

I've grown older, but life is good.
My adulthood.
My memories.
My reveries.

Masterpieces Found
Sheila Stephen

Trees sway in their dances
To nature's symphony
Seasons saunter in passage
As they appear casually

From the branches come voices
Of God's versatile birds
—A concerto exquisite
—A composition superb

The four-legged creatures
Heed with alerted ears
Hearing all of God's music
In surroundings so near

The spotlight shines brightly
God's sun is the beam
Highlighting precisely
Nature's grand artistry

Reflecting there on a log
Fallen by weathered strikes
Meditation comes easily
Like sleep stalking at night

The Write Connections

With eyes closed and breaths long
I give thanks for the love
That God used to create
This theatre from above

. . . With deer sipping at streamside
And worms digging below
The moon seeks its clearance
While toads hop to and fro . . .

This is where I thank God
It comes so naturally
To give thanks for a blessing
Esteemed especially

God finds me here often
Physically when able
. . . But in serene meditation
Always quite capable

Oh! the music arrangements
Arias rich in sound
Productions of grand voices
. . . Masterpieces I found

Mr. Martin
Bernadette Sukley

I first met my neighbor the night his house burned down.
He stood shocked, the horrid glow of flames reflecting on his face.
I asked if he was okay.
He thanked me for my concern.

Commuting from wreckage to work, he lived out of his car.
I baked him coffee cake and put it by his trunk.
He thanked me for the kindness.

They tore the rest of the house down. Not safe, you know . . .
I brought him tomatoes from my garden.
He thanked me for the produce.

He built three sheds and still lived out of his car.
I shared my little stray cat, who'd wander over to purr for him.
He thanked me for the companionship.

He rebuilt his house, not of sticks, but of bricks.
I placed a pumpkin on his new front stoop.
He nodded and smiled. We both knew my gifts were too little, too late.
He closed the door and hid behind his walls.

I dropped off Christmas cookies, warm wishes for the New Year.
He dropped off a card with a gold star, it said, *Thank you.*
It was signed: *Mr. Martin.*
I'll never know his first name. And he doesn't know mine.

The Write Connections

There are things we don't need to know about each other. Recluses and nosy neighbors aren't meant to be intertwined.

Lesson for a Young Nurse
Christine Talley

I move from one patient to the next,
dispensing pills, evaluating pains, checking the color of nail beds.

Suddenly, an elderly lady with shaky hands
gives me something small and hard.
I stare down and my palm stares back.

I was never taught in nursing school how to deal with this fragility.
A glass eye.

Okay, I'm calm,
breathe . . .

I'm calm.
I'm washing someone's eyeball.
Slippery glass above hard porcelain drain,
Leering at me as it swirls in my palm.
Okay, I'm calm.

Pop!
A grateful little woman smiles at me with both her eyes.

✝

Life Drained
Emily Thompson

My life had drained of color and excitement. I could barely see it.

She didn't remember the start of it.

The missing, then lost, spoken words.

Confrontations, at first discreet, then nonexistent.
How every day, turned into overcast, cloudy.
How others had turned blind and deaf to her.
Gray and dreary, even when it was sunny, blue skies.
How had she become dense, and ladened.
Too weighted down to get out of that chair to walk to the next way-station.
    See the next task.
Start the next task. Complete the next task.

When had she become just a page, a notation in someone's book?
A lingering deficient, there to hear and answer the calling page.
Was she just sojourning, craving atonement until that decisive page, which
    seems so imminent.
She had glimpsed it before, while standing in lines unnoticed.
Or on dark travels. Down empty streets, in eyes pale, hidden, colorless,
    glazed lost.

She had understood the concession of, *The Way It Was*. Now, she had
    glimpsed it for her life, abridged.
She too became lost, wandering streets vaguely remembered, mostly
    forgotten.

The Write Connections

Her father had gone gray and pasty.
Overlooked by all, and forgotten.
She didn't recall exactly when he disappeared;
when his voice and presence just dissolved away, while his body remained.

Her mother lasted a bit longer.
Until the decaying, graying of her mind began.
Her mother's dematerialization, would soon became complete.
She had hoped the condition would not be shared beyond her existence.
    That was not to be.

Passed by and ignored. Unless she protested. Cried out and demanded
    acknowledgment.
Rarely happened to others, those still bright and color-filled strangers.
Eyeing the mirror, she saw no reassuring reflection.
No, she remembered her parents. Their life had become subdued. Their
    color had drained.
She saw no light. Nor darkening prescience showed.
She had become invisible.

✝

Authors

Peggy Adamczyk

Peggy spent her childhood vacations traveling the east coast with her parents, visiting state parks and museums. She developed a love of history and recognized the correlation between present-day events and the past. Today Peggy uses that knowledge to explore human nature in the face of diversify in her writing. Peggy lives in the keystone state with an electronic junkie and three cats. She attended Warren County Community College and takes home-based college courses in various subjects including; History, Science, and Writing. Since 1994, she has been a member of member of Pennwriters INC and severed as secretary and president. She has been nominated three times for the Pennwriters Meritorious Service Award. In 1993, she became a founding member of Greater Lehigh Valley Writers Group. Peggy has held various GLVWG board positions over the years. This year she is serving her third term as president. She is published in newspapers, newsletters, anthologies, and plans to release her fist book in her trilogy soon. She also gives workshops at local events.

Beatriz Eugenia Arias

Beatriz is a new member of the Greater Lehigh Valley Writers Group. She's been writing since an early age. She's taking the first step into publishing with the 2017 GLVWG Anthology.

Beverly Botelho

Beverly is retired from the field of human services and has been writing poetry and creating collages since she was a child. Her poetry has been published in the *New York Times* and *Cedar Rock*. She has published a book of poetry *Angel, Mine*.

Mike Boushell

Mike taught Creative Writing, American Literature, and A.P. Composition and Grammar during his thirty-two year teaching career. In 1984 he received a Fellowship in Writing from the NEH, and has taught graduate level courses for Marywood College and Duquesne University. His first novel, *Freshman Flash,* was nominated for a Young Readers Choice Award by the PA School Librarians Association and was named to its Recommended Reading List for Middle School Students. His second novel, *Gridiron Hero,* was named to The Kansas State Reading Circle Recommended Reading List for Middle School Students. A member of GLVWG since his retirement from Education in 2001, Mike has had numerous poems published and has been an invited speaker at high schools, as well as teachers conferences and writers workshops. In 2003 he was an invited guest speaker on the well-know television show Daily News Live on the Comcast Sports Network in Philadelphia. He was also an invited speaker at the Pennsylvania Librarians Annual Conference in Hershey PA. His poem *50's Summer* was awarded first place in the 2014 GLVWG Open Poetry Competition. His novels are available at Barnes and Noble, Amazon and Royal Fireworks Publishing Company in Unionville, NY. He lives in Easton, PA, with his wife, Kathy, their dog Chloe Joe, and two adopted cats: Miss Kitty Cat Kat and the Calico Kid.

The Write Connections

Joy Crayton

Joy has been a member of the Phillipsburg Library's Coffee, Tea and Classics as well as The Happy Bookers book clubs for many years. Her love of reading and interest in writing led her to join an Easton area writers group and in 2014, her poetry and flash fiction appeared in *Final Draft Volume 2*, a locally published anthology. She joined the Greater Lehigh Valley Writers Group in 2015 and currently lives in the Lehigh Valley.

Ilissa Jae Ducoat

Ilissa has been writing since the second grade. In addition to being a mother of two fantastic children, she is also a Licensed Professional Counselor, specializing in grief and loss. Ilissa manages her agency's blog at alliancecounselingcenter.wordpress.com. She also has contributed pieces to Psych Central and Grief Digest online.

John Evans

John is a writer with a special interest in Mark Twain. In 1993, University Press of America published his first book, *A Tom Sawyer Companion* which explores Twain's boyhood. A short story, "Getting the Bugs out of Tom Sawyer," was included in Glencoe McGraw Hill's 2000 Literary Library edition of *Tom Sawyer*. He has also reviewed books for the Mark Twain Forum and has written articles and personal essays. In 2003, his first novel *The Cut* was published by Beachhouse Books. His first mystery, *A Dead*

Issue, was released by Sunbury Press in 2013. John has been a member of GLVWG since 1993 and has served as president, vice-president, and member representative. Currently he is the Author Advocacy Chair. He is also an active member of International Thriller Writers. John lives in an old farmhouse in Bangor, Pennsylvania with his wife, daughter, and things that go bump in the night.

Phil Giunta

Pennsylvania resident Phil graduated from Saint Joseph's University in Philadelphia with a Bachelor of Science in Information Systems back in the days when data was saved by chiseling it into stone. Phil continues to work in the IT industry, but honestly, he would love nothing more than to escape corporate America and open his own bait and tackle shop, or explore outer space in a starship, which might allow him to open a bait and tackle shop on another planet. At least he has a plan, but we digress . . . His first novel, a paranormal mystery called *Testing the Prisoner*, was published in 2010 by Firebringer Press. His second novel in the same genre, *By Your Side*, was released in 2013. Phil also narrated the audio versions of both novels, available for free at podiobooks.com/contributor/phil-giunta. Phil's short stories appear in such anthologies as *Beach Nights* from Cat and Mouse Press, the *ReDeus* series from Crazy 8 Press, and the *Middle of Eternity* series, which he created and edited for Firebringer Press. His paranormal mystery novella, *Like Mother, Like Daughters* is slated for release in 2017. Phil is a member of the Greater Lehigh Valley Writers Group and served as chairman of their 2015 Write Stuff conference. Visit Phil's website at: www.philgiunta.com.

The Write Connections

Keith Keffer

Keith is an author, software developer, martial artist and an avid gamer. His earliest writing revolved around writing adventure games, and three decades later that effort led to the completion of his first novel. He is the author of three novels: *Shaper of Stone, Shaper of Air* and *Shaper of Fire*. His short story, *372*, was included in Laurel Highlands Publishing's anthology *Disturbance*. *Mementos* marks the third year that Keith has contributed to the Greater Lehigh Valley Writers Group annual anthology. Keith loves books, lots of books in lots of different genres. He tends to be an action/adventure type junkie. If it has monsters, swords, magic, explosions, spaceships, ghosts or cowboys he is probably going to enjoy it. He is also a sucker for crude, twisted humor. Keith claims that it's not his fault. His dad led him to the dark side many years ago. He tries to keep it reigned in, but it's like the Hulk. Once it is out, it is hard to get it back under control. You can find out more about Keith by visiting his website, keithkeffer.com or by emailing him at keith@keithkeffer.com.

Charles Kiernan

Retired from gainful employment, Charles pursues storytelling and writing. He leans toward the oral telling of fairy tales in his performances and the fantasy realm in his novels, but prefers 'off-center realism' for his short stories. He is president of the Lehigh Valley Storytelling Guild, Pennsylvania State Representative for the National Youth Storytelling Showcase, Pennsylvania State Liaison for the National Storytelling Network and recipient of the 2008 Individual Artist Award from the Bethlehem Fine Arts Commission. He has been the Chair of the Write Stuff Writers Conference for 2016 and 2017. He has an international readership with his blog, *Fairy Tale of the Month,* which he has produced faithfully every month since December of 2010.

Jennifer Lader

Jennifer finds stories wherever she goes. As an award-winning writer and editor, she helps people and businesses share their stories and meet their goals. She is a speaker, instructor and coach, and active in the Lehigh Valley Storytelling Guild. Jennifer lives in Bethlehem, Pennsylvania, with her husband and three children. Visit her at: jenniferlader.com.

Gisela Leck

Gisela grew up in Southern Germany before making the United States her permanent home. She studied at the University of Texas at Austin as well as the University of Minnesota at Minneapolis where she earned an M.S.W. Gisela lives in Bethlehem, PA, and teaches sociology at a local college. She loves writing and has recently completed several short stories and a novel. Her interests are many, including reading, acting, hiking, rowing, traveling, going to the movies, and trying out new recipes. For Gisela, nothing beats getting to spend time with her husband and daughter.

Robert Martin

Robert's writings have appeared in *Mature Years*; *Alive Now*; *Wilderness*

House Literary Review; and *Long Story Short*, among others. He won two *Faith and Hope* awards and wrote two chapbooks. His favorite hobby is watching his beloved NY Giants play football. His main writing influences are Kahil Gibran and Pablo Neruda.

Suzanne Grieco Mattaboni

Suzanne is a fiction writer, blogger, poet and corporate PR consultant based in Northampton, Pennsylvania. Author of the middle grade novel *Taco Girl* and the new adult novel *Excuse Me, Waitress, Is That New Jersey?*, she is a former community service and education reporter for *Newsday*. Her work has appeared in *Seventeen*, The *Chicken Soup for the Soul* anthologies, The Huffington Post, *Mysterious Ways*, Guideposts.com, *Child*, 50 Word Stories, SixWordMemoirs.com, *Turtle*, *Humpty Dumpty's*, *The Best of LA Parent*, the *What's a Nice Girl Like You Doing in a Relationship Like This?* anthology, and a host of high tech trade magazines. She's a past winner of *Seventeen* magazine's Art and Fiction Contest. Originally from Long Island, New York, she has a B.A. in fiction writing from the University of Pittsburgh and studied literature and art at the City of London Polytechnic. Suzanne has generated public relations coverage with *The New York Times*, *Bloomberg News*, *The Wall Street Journal*, *The New York Post*, *BusinessWeek*, *The Philadelphia Inquirer*, *The Phoenix Business Journal* and other major business publications across North America. Visit her at copywritelife.com or on Twitter: @suzmattaboni.

The Write Connections

Veronica Mattaboni

Veronica is a fiction and poetry author from Pennsylvania. She graduated from West Chester University of Pennsylvania with a B.A. in English Writing and a minor in Creative Writing. Veronica's work has been featured on the *Feminine Collective*, Penn and Anvil Press, *Heart Beings*, and *Daedalus*. She has also worked as an Associate Editor with 823 on High, and as Editor in Chief of Literati.

Jerome W. McFadden

Jerome has been writing fiction for the past seven years. His stories have appeared in various magazines, and e-zines such as *Flash Fiction Offensive, Over My Dead Body, Eclectic Flash Fiction* and *BWG Writers Round Table*. He received a second place Bullet Award for the Best Crime Fiction to appear on the web in June 2011 and had his short stories read aloud on the stage by the Liars' League in London and the Liars' League in Hong Kong. His stories have also appeared in various anthelia including, *Hard Boiled: Crime Scene*; *Deep, Dark Woods*; *One Star Reviews of the Afterlife; Write Here, Write Now; Once Around the Sun, A Christmas Sampler, A Readable Feast* and *Let it Snow*.

Donna Searle McLay

Donna is a former teacher, reading specialist, and principal who specializes in writing. She studied teaching of writing and memoir at Columbia, and is a Fellow of the Pennsylvania Writing and Literature Project and the National Writing Project. She has a studio in the GoggleWorks Center for the Arts in Reading, PA, where she holds writing workshops and teaches occasional classes. She is the mother of four and grandmother of eleven.

David A. Miller, II

David is a member of GLVWG, has published *Time Birds,* a spy adventure sci-fi novel available on Amazon's Kindle and Barnes & Noble. In work: *Time Birds: The Phoenix,* the second novel in this trilogy. Almost complete: *Bravo 26.* This fast-paced thriller details the revenge, adventures and mistakes of a Special Forces unit. He has also written *A Gift of Love*, a history of the Lutheran Home at Topton, PA.

Susan Kling Monroe

Susan is a Pennsylvania librarian, and has been making up and writing tales all of her life. Her book reviews have been published in *Wild Violet*, the on-line literary magazine. This is her first anthology.

Florence Morton

Florence launched her writing career at a memoir writing class, held over ten years ago, at the former "Writer's Room" in Doylestown, Pa. She holds a special interest in writing memoir. She is an educator by training, having over 40 years of combined experience in teaching and supervision and administration of educational programs and continues to write and participate in critique groups. She loves writing as an expression of self, as well as through the camaraderie and idea exchange of fellow writers during critique.

☐

Christopher D. Ochs

Chris' foray into writing began in 2014 with his self-published epic fantasy, *Pindlebryth of Lenland: The Five Artifacts*, recommended by US Review of Books. Several of his short stories have been published in the Greater Lehigh Valley Writers Group and Bethlehem Writers Group anthologies and websites. His latest work is a collection of mirthful macabre short stories, *If I Can't Sleep, You Can't Sleep*. His current literary projects include: more short tales of the weird; a backstory novella e-book and the second novel in the *Pindlebryth* saga. If all that weren't enough to keep him busy, Chris is active in several groups spanning writing, storytelling and anime fandom ("Voice of OTAKON"). It's a wonder he can remember to pay the dog and feed his bills. Wait, what?

☐

Bart Palamaro

Bart has been an IT professional for thirty years. He started Dark Horse Productions, a video productions company specializing in shooting commercial and training videos. Feeling unchallenged he started doing 2D and 3D animation and computer graphics. Along the way, he wrote two novels and is working on a third. With the indie publishing revolution in full swing he learned to format books for print and eBooks using only MS Word. This way he can make others' books real. He's done a few dozen books and does cover art as well.

☐

The Write Connections

Richard Rosinski

Richard is a former professor, researcher, and computer executive who has published several dozen technical articles and seven non-fiction books. He is the coauthor of five computer books that sold over 178,000 copies. More recently, his writing has turned to techno-procedural fiction, focusing on social connections in technical work environments.

Larry Sceurman

Larry has been telling stories for more than twenty-five years. He has evolved from a street performer and stand-up comic into an enchanting storyteller. Being a proud member and co-founder of the Lehigh Valley Storytelling Guild has helped him to understand the importance and need of story. He is now putting his skills and creativity into the printed word with short stories, poems and snippets of life. Larry is influenced by the writings of Laura E. Richards, John O'Connor, Richard Ford and Billy Collins.

Dawn M. Sooy

Dawn worked as a Business Analyst in the Telecommunications area. This included writing training material for each program launched. One major launch this telecommunications company supported was the first generation iPhone. She wrote the documentation for training the agents to work the orders. In 2014, she decided to resign from her job and begin writing again. In between writing short stories, she is currently working on a novel *New Beginnings*. Recent short story publications include: *Bed Partners*, Queer Sci-Fi Publishing; *Vital Signs*, Torque Publishing; *Holly's Ghost*, Zimbell House Publishing LLC; *Katie's Wish*, James Ward Kirk Publishing. She serves as the Greater Lehigh Valley Writers Group's secretary over 2015-2016. Her website is dmsooy.wix.com/dmsooyauthor.

Sheila Stephen

Sheila has been writing for as long as she can remember! Her serious attempts at writing began when she was 36. Her work includes short stories, lots of poetry, and even a novel from which she gained great experience at handling rejection slips. Some pieces of her poetry printed here and there, but most of her work benefits the members of her church via its newsletter. About twenty years ago she began crafting her own greeting cards and including her poetry, just to get it out there. She's participated in a devotional publication for her church and would love to someday do more in that area. She discovered GLVWG on the internet and has begun attending meetings to hone her skills.

Bernadette Sukley

Bernadette has been researching, writing, and editing for over twenty-five years. Her work has appeared in newsletters, newspapers, magazines and books. She's edited sports, health, and lifestyle publications, and she's interviewed Olympians and politicians. She's also done research for medical associations and hospitals. She's compiled content for every sort of publication from medical brochures to marathon calendars. She's been a vet tech, babysitter, aerobics instructor, and a nurse's aide. Her first book, *A Saving Hurricane* was self-published in 2008. Her second novel, *Find Me a Woman* was published in 2014. Her first nonfiction, *Made in Pennsylvania* came out last year. When she's not writing, she's running, watching nature, or trying to make something pretty, tasty, or cool. Visit her at thequirkywriter.blogspot.com or bernadettewsukley.com.

Christine Talley

Christine is a wife and mother of two sons. As Clotilda Warhammer of Mistwraithe Hall, she was a sword and shield fighter in the Society for Creative Anachronism (SCA), a medieval re-enactment group, for nine years. She participated in numerous battles, along with a thousand other fighters, during nine Pennsic Wars and other events, when she wasn't working as a registered nurse. She drew upon these experiences to write her first, self-published novel, *The Girl in the Bird: Romance and Alien Power in the Current Middle Ages,* which is primarily set during events of the SCA. She has written poetry for many years, pulling from her life experiences and has participated in three NaNoWriMo's (National Novel Writing Month) winning in 2015 with her novel.

Emily Thompson

Emily writes and works in a doctor's office. She's been many things and had many different jobs, unrelated to writing. She's published short stories in the Greater Lehigh Valley Writers Group's 2015 and 2016 anthologies *GLVWG Writes Stuff* and *Write Here, Write Now* and published a short story in *Goldfinch* Women Who Write publication. She writes under the pen name, T.A. Searforth. She writes because it allows her to explore the world she lives in, and the world her mind sees. Writing frustrates and vexes her, and gives her great pleasure all at the same time.

Rachel Thompson

Rachel is a freelance writer who wrote for the Lehigh Valley News Group two years as a beat reporter and feature writer, along with two columns, Artist Muse and Construction Guru. Her freelance work includes press packages and PR work for human rights and GLBT rights organizations, local and national magazines, cartoon work for magazines, newsprint, and greeting card companies. Previously in construction management, she occasionally wrote for trade publications and published short stories. She now concentrates on fiction but periodically writes for magazines. She has written three novels, a nonfiction manuscript and forty short stories. She will self publish an anthology of twenty-one short stories in 2017 called *Stalking Kilgore Trout*.

Diane VanDyke

Whether she is writing a blog entry, short story or feature article, Diane is in her creative zone when she connects words and sentences to paint a lasting image and share a good story. Her writing adventures started in her teenage years but then were put aside and rediscovered a decade later when she started writing for her hometown newspaper. Her freelance assignments led to a part-time staff position and then to a full-time editorial position with

Berks-Mont Newspapers. Eventually, she followed the path of marketing and public relations for Montgomery County Community College, where she currently uses her writing skills today. Beyond writing, Diane likes to run, read, bike and enjoy the beauty of sunrises and sunsets.

Carol L. Wright

Carol is a former lawyer and academic who traded writing law related topics for writing fiction. She has published several short stories and is currently at work on a murder mystery set in the Berkshire foothills of Massachusetts . She is a member of Sisters in Crime, the Jane Austen Society of North America, the Bethlehem Writers Group, Pennwriters, and SinC Guppies. She is married to her college sweetheart and lives in the Lehigh Valley. Visit her at: carollwright.com or on Facebook at bit.ly/2jGmsMj.

Visit glvwg.org and
join the
Greater Lehigh Valley Writers Group

We would be happy to help you publish
in our next anthology!

Made in United States
North Haven, CT
04 August 2022

22224860R00114